"You said you wanted lessons in being carefree, Raine....

"Welcome to Easy-Going 202," Mitch said.

"I was kidding."

"Were you?"

Joey's plastic cup hit the floor, then bounced twice, spraying orange liquid in every direction. He took one look at Mitch, started to cry and made a nosedive for Raine's lap.

Raine automatically cuddled Joey, meeting Mitch's gaze over the toddler's blond head.

"You've probably noticed I could use a few pointers on child care," Mitch said.

Looking at his cluttered home and at the serious-eyed child on her lap, Raine answered, "I'd say what you need even more is a wife."

His silence drew her gaze. "Are you applying for the job?"

Dear Reader,

This month, Silhouette Romance brings you six wonderful new love stories—guaranteed to keep your summer sizzling! Starting with a terrific FABULOUS FATHER by Arlene James. A *Mail-order Brood* was not what Leon Paradise was expecting when he asked Cassie Esterbridge to be his wife. So naturally the handsome rancher was shocked when he discovered that his mail-order bride came with a ready-made family!

Favorite author Suzanne Carey knows the kinds of stories Romance readers love. And this month, Ms. Carey doesn't disappoint. *The Male Animal* is a humorous tale of a couple who discover love—in the midst of their divorce.

The fun continues as Marie Ferrarella brings us another delightful tale from her Baby's Choice series—where matchmaking babies bring together their unsuspecting parents.

In an exciting new trilogy from Sandra Steffen, the Harris brothers vow that no woman will ever tie them down. But their WEDDING WAGER doesn't stand a chance against love. This month, a confirmed bachelor suddenly becomes a single father—and a more-than-willing groom—in *Bachelor Daddy*.

Rounding out the month, Jeanne Rose combines the thrill of the chase with the excitement of romance in *Love on the Run*. And *The Bridal Path* is filled with secrets—and passion—as Alaina Hawthorne spins a tale of love under false pretenses.

I hope you'll join us in the coming months for more great books from Elizabeth August, Kasey Michaels and Helen Myers.

Until then—

Happy Reading!

Anne Canadeo
Senior Editor

Please address questions and book requests to:
Silhouette Reader Service
U.S.: 3010 Walden Ave., P.O. Box 1325, Buffalo, NY 14269
Canadian: P.O. Box 609, Fort Erie, Ont. L2A 5X3

BACHELOR DADDY

Sandra Steffen

Silhouette
R O M A N C E™
Published by Silhouette Books
America's Publisher of Contemporary Romance

For Orva & Doug Reed,
whose very lives prove that love happens
when we least expect it

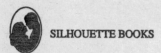 SILHOUETTE BOOKS

ISBN 0-373-19028-X

BACHELOR DADDY

Copyright © 1994 by Sandra E. Steffen

Printed in U.S.A.

SANDRA STEFFEN

Creating memorable characters is one of Sandra's favorite aspects of writing. She's always been a romantic, and is thrilled to be able to spend her days doing what she loves—bringing her characters to life on her computer screen.

Sandra grew up in Michigan, the fourth of ten children, all of whom have taken the old adage "Go forth and multiply" quite literally. Add to this her husband, who is her real-life hero, their four school-age sons who keep their lives in constant motion, their gigantic cat, Percy, and her wonderful friends, in-laws and neighbors, and what do you get? Chaos, of course, but also a wonderful sense of belonging she wouldn't trade for the world.

We, the undersigned, do hereby declare our state of bachelorhood to be a sacred trust. We shall in no way attempt to endanger our single status by dating seriously, fathering a child or—heaven forbid—falling in love. He who does not abide by this contract shall be banished from the brotherhood of bachelors for all time.

This contract we do honor. Let no woman place a ring upon our finger.

Kyle Harris

Mitch Harris

Taylor Harris

Chapter One

Raine stepped up to the bar and slid onto the high stool. Hooking the heel of one shoe over the rung, she crossed her legs and glanced at her watch. She was early. With a buoyancy brought on by inner happiness, she realized it didn't matter. There was nothing she *had* to do, nothing to hurry off to, no one to worry about but herself.

"What'll it be, sweetheart?"

She nearly giggled out loud, and Raine McAlister didn't giggle. Men didn't call her sweetheart, and the last time she'd had a drink was at the office Christmas party last year when Mildred Crandel in personnel had brought in a batch of Fuzzy Navels, a horrendous-sounding drink that tasted like peachy orange juice. That drink was fine for an office party, but this was not a Fuzzy Navel kind of night.

"Well," she pondered, "I *am* celebrating. Perhaps a glass of white wine."

"If you're celebrating, I'd recommend something with a little more celebration in it, like champagne, or sparkling burgundy."

The bartender raised his thick eyebrows, and Raine thought he wouldn't have made a bad Humphrey Bogart. "Sparkling burgundy sounds perfect."

While she waited for her drink, she cast a covert glance at the man seated to her left. Lost in thought, he stared into a squat glass that held an amber liquid. The poor guy looked miserable, as miserable as a broad-shouldered, arrestingly attractive man could look. He didn't glance up, not even when the bartender placed a long-stemmed glass in front of her and moved on to his next customer, leaving Raine alone to swirl the wine in her gears and wait for her friends to arrive.

She took a sip and the wine's tiny bubbles tickled her lips and slid over her tongue like excitement. It was too bad her happiness wasn't contagious. Mr. Lonesome could have used a large dose. Although he looked like a man with reason to drown his sorrows, he still hadn't lifted the glass to his lips.

Edging closer, she murmured, "Think it would help to talk about it?"

The man turned his head slowly, and she chastised herself for interfering. After visiting her parents' graves and standing in the warm rain this afternoon, she felt reborn. Her brother and sister were both in college, and Raine was free. But she never could ignore someone in need. She'd nursed more stray animals back to health than she could remember, and human beings, well, they were impossible to turn away, the promise she'd made to herself about becoming more carefree notwithstanding.

Raine's newly awakened sense of life surged through her as she met the man's look. Even though he hadn't raised his chin, his gaze didn't rove below her shoulders before climbing higher the way so many men's did. He looked directly into her eyes, and she found that his were the bluest she'd ever seen. Like pools of appeal, his gaze held hers, dipped to her mouth, then back again. In that moment, he didn't seem anything like a stray.

Lifting her glass, she whispered, "To the future."

The man wrapped his hand around his glass and clinked it against hers. "Yeah, sure, to the future."

Mesmerized, she watched his lips part, watched the muscle in his neck move as the whiskey slid down his throat. By the time his eyes met hers again, his had warmed about twenty degrees. She might have attributed it to the whiskey, had it not been for the draw of his gaze and the slow tingling in her own stomach.

"A bad day?" she asked. After all, he'd probably just had a huge argument with his wife. She checked his left hand, his *bare* left hand. Maybe he'd lost his job. Maybe he thought it was none of her business, which was true, yet Raine couldn't help it. People in need drew her.

But this man looked troubled, not needy. He was compelling, in a laid-back sort of way, and the slow, raking gaze he gave her made her even more curious.

For the second time in a few short hours, Mitch Harris felt as if he'd been hit with a ton of bricks. The first had knocked the wind out of him, the second had put it back again. This woman's sultry voice drew his gaze. Her brown eyes and pert nose, the blond wisps of hair framing her face and feathering her ears drew the rest of him.

He wasn't easily shaken. In fact, most upheavals rolled right off him. But the registered letter he'd received from an attorney in Arizona had been staggering. Mitch had no idea how long he'd been staring into his drink, and hell, he knew he'd been accused of being forgetful a time or two, but his mind had never been wiped clean at the first sight of a beautiful woman.

"My name's Raine McAlister, and if you want to talk about it, I'm a great listener."

"Rain, like a storm?" he asked.

Her smile was soft, her laughter slightly wistful. "No. Storms are exciting, and I haven't exactly led an exciting life."

He watched her swirl her wine, twirling the glass's thin stem between her fingers. Her hands were narrow, her fingers long and slender, her nails tapered and unpainted. Nothing about her was blatant, certainly not her gray slacks and white blouse, her gold watch or those tiny gold earrings peeking through her short hair. But her eyes sparkled with inner happiness and her smile was soft as dew.

That last swig of whiskey had warmed his stomach. The slender elbow brushing his arm warmed the rest of him. She didn't seem like the type of woman who sat in bars and picked up men. In fact, if this was a come-on, he'd bite glass.

"Come here often?" she asked.

Mitch swallowed a good portion of his drink and tried to get his mind off her mouth. Since he doubted she'd appreciate being dragged by her hair to the nearest cave, he tramped down his initial response to her.

"No. How about you?"

"Actually, I haven't gotten out much lately." Leaning closer, she whispered, "Have you ever felt on the brink of a whole new life?"

Her words smacked like a fist to his jaw and he was reminded of his reason for coming here tonight. "You could say that."

"Oh, dear," she murmured. "You don't look nearly as thrilled about your new life as I am about mine."

"Yeah, well, I'm still in a state of shock over mine."

"I know exactly what you need."

Mitch waited with bated breath. *Your cave or mine?*

"You need to have some fun."

He figured that was a start. "What sort of fun do you have when your troubles get you down?"

"What do I do?" Joy bubbled in her laugh and sparkled in her eyes. "Something light, something free. An airplane ride, or a trip to the mountains. Do something you love, and I guarantee you'll find your perspective."

Mitch was already finding his perspective. He already knew what he wanted, and it had nothing to do with that letter from Arizona. This woman sent an awareness he hadn't felt in years strumming through him. Any other day, he would have given in to instinct and whispered a kiss along her lips. But not tonight. Tonight, he had more to think about than just himself.

Touching his glass to hers, he said, "To new beginnings."

Raine took a sip of wine. *To new beginnings.* She wondered if he had any idea how appropriate his words were. She was about to tell him, but before she could put her thoughts into words, two women flailing their arms at her across the room drew her attention.

She dropped a bill on the counter and slid from the bar stool. "My friends just arrived. It's been nice talking to you, er..."

"Mitch. Mitch Harris," he said with a slow, thoughtful smile.

Raine watched what that smile of his did to his face, and felt what it did to her. Not only was he good-looking, he had a great physique, and a problem, a big one if the worry in his eyes was any indication. She was probably lucky her friends had arrived when they did, or she might have given in to her temptation to lend a helping hand. As it was, all she had time to do was murmur, "Don't forget. Do something you love and you'll figure out what to do about the rest."

Mitch watched her cast him one last look before she disappeared through a wide doorway. Do something he loved to do, huh? At that moment, what he wanted to do more than anything was follow Raine through that doorway.

Instead, he downed the rest of his drink, took a bill from his wallet and slowly slid from the stool. He'd been too preoccupied to get her phone number, but absentminded or not, he doubted he'd ever forget that smile. She'd said her name was Raine McAlister. He wasn't likely to forget that, either, or the way her sensuality had drawn him from his deep thoughts. No, he wouldn't forget Raine. Not in a million years.

Mitch stole the basketball from Taylor, then stormed back to the hoop. It had been a rainy Saturday morning, and the driveway was slick with moisture. The ball swished through the net before either of his brothers could block the shot. "Pay attention, guys. That was game point, and I won. Again. Come on, let's play another game."

"Forget it," Kyle, older than Mitch by a mere fourteen months, grumbled.

"What's with you?" Taylor, younger by a year, dribbled the ball on the wet concrete to accent his question. "You're killin' us today." With that, he flung the ball at Mitch and pursued their former conversation. "I'm telling you, it's time for a new bet."

"Oh, no. That trophy's mine," Kyle answered. "Neither of you will ever be able to top that astronaut I dated a couple years ago."

Mitch didn't participate in the discussion. The fact that he'd heard it all before had little to do with it. He'd been keyed up all weekend, and it was only Saturday. He'd taken Raine's advice, driving straight from that bar in Allentown to Taylor's apartment in Philadelphia, intent on playing a hard game of basketball with his brothers, something he normally enjoyed. For once, physical exertion hadn't helped. Tension still knotted his shoulders, pounded in his temples.

Holding the ball in the crook of one arm, he listened to his brothers' conversation. They'd had a standing bet for over twenty years, this one not much different than all the rest. Juvenile. They were all in their mid-thirties, and both his brothers were still juvenile. Compared to his problem, their silly bets seemed petty and insignificant.

"I think," Taylor persisted, "that whoever has enough nerve to show up at the folks' anniversary party later this fall with a woman should win the trophy."

"Too easy," Kyle jeered. "Let's make it interesting, add a rider. It can't be just any woman."

Mitch shook his head. "Why don't you insist we show up with a wife, for heaven's sake?"

Kyle grabbed the ball from Mitch's hand and spun it on his finger. "You're on! Whoever shows up with a wife, or a fiancée," he amended, "wins the trophy, permanently."

"Where do you intend to find a wife or a fiancée?" Mitch asked.

"You're a dentist," Kyle replied to his brother's question. "Don't good-looking women ever sit in your chair and say ah?"

"Dentists' patients don't say ah." Mitch had the presence of mind to wonder if he sounded as juvenile as Kyle and Taylor.

"Try the laundromat." Taylor grinned. "I'm not kidding. A friend of mine swears he meets interesting women there. I've always had better luck in grocery stores."

"Forget it," Mitch said. "The bet's off."

"You're outnumbered," Kyle cut in. "Two to one. The bet stands."

After a long moment of deliberation, Mitch said, "I have a better idea. I say the first one who becomes a father should hold the trophy. Permanently."

The basketball slipped from Kyle's hand and bounced through a puddle farther down the driveway. No one moved to retrieve it. Mitch's statement had wiped the smiles from his brothers' faces, but then, he wasn't smiling, either.

"Now that I have your attention, I have something to tell you." The problem was, he didn't know how to begin. He settled his hands on his hips as he looked from Taylor's face to Kyle's, and back again. "I wasn't going to mention this. I wanted to talk to a lawyer first."

"What the hell's going on?" Kyle sputtered.

"What lawyer?" Taylor asked.

Mitch took another deep breath then let it all out in one long-suffering sigh. "I received a letter yesterday. From an attorney in Arizona. Someone died. A woman..."

"A woman you knew?" Taylor asked.

"Briefly." Mitch met their *I'll just bet* expressions.

Taylor asked, "What does that have to do with going to see an attorney?"

"She mentioned me in her will."

"What did she leave you?" Kyle's eyes narrowed a little more with every word.

"She left me her son. My son."

The same four-letter word slid from Taylor's and Kyle's mouths. The word, unbecoming but extremely eloquent under the circumstances, hung between them for several seconds. Kyle was the first to find his voice. "What are you going to do about it?"

"*Him*, Kyle. What am I going to do about *him*." Mitch ran his hand through his hair before continuing. "I'm going to find out if it's true, if he's really mine. And if he is, I'm going to bring him home."

This time, neither Kyle nor Taylor said a word. Staring into their shocked faces, Mitch knew exactly how they felt.

He strode to the center of the driveway and scooped up the basketball from a shallow puddle. After bouncing it in his brothers' general direction, he straightened his spine and turned toward the street.

"Where are you going?" Taylor asked.

Without breaking stride, Mitch answered, "For a drive."

"Want some company?"

Mitch looked back at them and slowly shook his head. "Not this time. I have to figure out this situation for myself. I'll let you know what I decide to do."

Taylor and Kyle stayed where they were on the wet driveway, watching as Mitch drove away. Long after he'd disappeared from view, Taylor finally whispered, "A kid."

"Yeah," Kyle answered. "A kid."

Mitch rubbed his blurry eyes, feeling so exhausted he barely knew which end was up. He hadn't waited until Monday to see an attorney, after all. It turned out Taylor had a friend who practiced law, whom Mitch went to see the next day. He hadn't cared if the guy charged him triple time because it was Sunday; this matter was too important to wait, even one more day. Mitch had flown to Arizona on Sunday where, luckily, the paperwork was handled quickly, allowing Mitch to return home on Tuesday.

A movement drew Mitch's gaze. Across the room, the child, his child, was sleeping in the big recliner. This was the first time the boy had slept since his arrival yesterday. One thumb was in his mouth and the other scrunched a tattered blanket.

So many feelings welled up inside Mitch, he couldn't begin to name them all. Staring at his son, every protective instinct in Mitch's body surged through him, along with every feeling of inadequacy he possessed.

Elizabeth had named her baby Joseph James Russell. But Mitch had already begun the proper legal steps to give the boy his own last name. In Mitch's eyes, Joey was already a Harris.

If the past four days had been the longest in Mitch's life, it was nothing compared to how they must have seemed to Joey. He'd known from the beginning the boy was only two. His cousins had two-year-olds, and those kids hadn't seemed all that young. But hell, those kids weren't his, and Joey was little more than a baby. It hadn't taken Mitch long to figure out he knew a lot less about babies than he'd realized.

Taylor thought they should have called their parents home from Hawaii, where they were vacationing, but Mitch figured that among the three of them, they had over one hundred years of knowledge, and shouldn't have too much trouble handling one two-year-old. Watching Joey suck his thumb in his sleep, Mitch now realized the error in that kind of thinking.

His brothers had been great throughout the entire ordeal, going with him to see Taylor's attorney friend, offering to fly out to Arizona with him. Mitch had turned down their offer. He'd known it was going to be hard enough for his son's maternal grandmother to release Joey to a total stranger, without having to meet the child's two bachelor uncles, as well.

Mitch was glad he'd followed his instincts. Eva Russell, Joey's grandmother, was a seventy-four-year-old widow in failing health. She was as stubborn as a mule, but it was obvious she cared very deeply for her only grandson, and just as obvious she mourned the loss of her daughter. Tears had coursed down her cheeks when Mitch had carried a terrified Joey from her house. Mitch had felt just as terrified.

Joey's thumb fell from his mouth, and he jerked in his sleep. Mitch tensed, poised for action. He didn't take another breath until the child instinctively found his thumb again and settled back into a relaxed sleep.

Slumping in his chair, Mitch figured he should try to sleep, too. After all, who knew when the little boy would decide to rest again. But he was too nervous to sleep. He looked around at his cluttered home and knew his life wasn't the only thing turned upside down these past four days. He'd taken the week off from work, but it was already Wednesday, and he needed a plan, one that would encompass the next twenty years or so.

Somewhere in this plan, he intended to find Raine Mc-Alister, to look into her eyes and see if his memories were playing tricks on him, if her eyes were really brimming with promises of sensuality and with an inner energy she could barely contain.

Mitch checked on Joey, then tiptoed from the room. His dog, Tanner, lifted his head and looked forlornly at him through the sliding glass door. The poor animal didn't understand why he'd been banned from the house, and Mitch didn't know how to make him understand. He didn't know how to explain that his son was afraid of dogs, that he was afraid of his new uncles. Most of all, Mitch didn't know how to explain that Joey was afraid of his own father.

Minutes later, after stepping from what had to be the shortest shower in history, Mitch had a plan to make friends with his son, at least for the day. He only hoped Joey wasn't afraid of parks.

"Small world."

A tingle of recognition shivered over Raine at the sound of Mitch's voice. She'd told herself she'd imagined the way his voice melted her insides. She wasn't imagining it now. She brought her gaze down from her kite, her lips already beginning to lift into a smile, her lashes beginning to flutter down. Those same lashes flew back up at the sight of the towheaded toddler in Mitch's arms.

"I thought people only flew kites in the spring."

"Most people do," she answered, looking back into the sky. "That's why mine is the only kite in the sky tonight." If she thought he'd looked worried the last time she saw him, today he looked positively exhausted. She wondered how long it had been since he'd slept, wondered if the child on his hip had anything to do with his *problem*. Without looking down, she asked, "Who's your friend?"

He waited until she looked at him, taking his time answering even then. "This is my son, Joey."

His son? He couldn't have surprised her more if he'd told her he was from Mars. Several thoughts scrambled through Raine's mind, flitting away in confusion. One thought stayed. *She had no business being attracted to a married man.*

A tan-colored dog at Mitch's side chose that moment to whine. "And this is my dog, Tanner. Tanner, say hello to Raine." The dog immediately barked a friendly greeting.

Raine turned her head just in time to see the dog place his front paws on Mitch's hip. Joey whimpered and lunged for her arms. She somehow managed to catch him and meet Mitch's gaze at the same time. The child buried his head in her shoulder, clutching her neck as tight as he could.

"You're safe," she murmured over and over, enfolding the little boy securely in her embrace. "Tanner won't hurt you."

Mitch wasn't surprised Raine's voice was working magic on Joey's fears. It was having a similar effect of him. She was beautiful, in the softest, most feminine way imaginable. She was so slender, yet she effortlessly held the child in her arms.

"Look, Joey," she said softly, pointing into the sky, "kite." The wind yanked on the kite, and for the first time, Mitch saw his son's lips lift into a smile. That little smile sent an odd twinge to his heart.

"Kite," Joey repeated.

Mitch shook his head. It was the first word the child had spoken in four days, and for the first time since Sunday, Mitch thought this situation had better than half a chance of turning out okay. He wondered what kind of chance he had with Raine.

"Maybe Daddy will buy you a kite," she assured the little boy.

"Daddy?" Joey asked.

Swallowing the lump in his throat, Mitch looked into his son's face. Placing his fingers to his own chest, he said, "Daddy."

Raine's eyes met his over the top of Joey's head. He read the questions in her gaze, and hell, he didn't blame her. He barely understood what was going on, himself. All he knew for sure was that Joey was his son.

A gust of wind jerked her arm up, reminding them of the kite in the sky. "Are you divorced, Mitch?" she asked.

"Been a bachelor all my life."

"I see," she replied, but Mitch doubted she really understood. He wasn't even sure he knew how to explain it to her. But he wanted to try.

"I saw some swings and a sandbox over that hill. Maybe we could talk while Joey plays."

She settled Joey to her hip and nodded. Mitch took the kite from her hands and began to wind the string around the spool, smiling as Joey laughed at the way it soared through the sky. It made one final attempt to pull from his grasp, its tail curling behind it, then made a nosedive. In seconds it crashed to the ground, a tangled heap of string and plastic.

"Uh-oh," Mitch mumbled.

"Uh-oh," Joey repeated.

Raine shrugged her shoulders and said, "I lose more kites this way."

Mitch was entranced by the expression in Raine's eyes. He tried to smile, but, taking a step closer, his gaze dropped to her mouth, and all thoughts of smiling deserted him.

Raine watched his eyes travel over her face, watched it settle on her mouth, and knew a tingling on her own lips. She felt it each time she looked at him, felt on the brink of something wonderful. The child wiggled in her arms, then turned to stare into her face.

"He has your eyes," she whispered gravely.

"I know," he answered. "I know."

Without further conversation, they walked to the kite, Mitch's dog following close behind. All three peered over at the mangled kite, as if inspecting it for some sign of life. She set Joey on his feet and, scooping the remains of the Blue Falcon kite into her hands, marched to the nearest trash can and tossed it inside.

Raine stayed near the trash can and tried to make sense of the situation. When they had met, he'd said he had some problem. And here he was with a little boy he claimed was his son but who obviously didn't know what to call his own father. The child was terrified of the family dog, and wary of Mitch. Mitch said he'd been a bachelor all his life, yet here was his son. He had a problem, all right. No wonder he'd been staring into his drink when she first met him.

Glancing back, Raine saw that Joey was standing where she'd left him, a short distance away. He seemed to have forgotten some of his fear. Even though he wasn't participating in the activities, he wasn't crying, either. The little boy seemed content to watch as his father tried to wrestle a rubber ball from Tanner's clenched jaw. And Raine couldn't help admire the way Joey's father's faded jeans clung to his hips and thighs or the way his knit shirt clung to his back and shoulders.

This was only the second time she'd seen Mitch. But both times she'd sensed something lazily seductive in his expression. And both times she'd felt an immediate and total attraction.

The dog growled playfully and Mitch answered his pet with low growls of his own. Tanner dropped the ball at Mitch's feet and waited for him to hurtle it into the distance. With Tanner off and running, Mitch took Joey's hand, and visibly sighed with relief when the child didn't pull away.

He turned, his eyes meeting hers, and the place surrounding her heart swelled at his expression. He looked exhausted, but it didn't detract from the contemplative longing in his eyes. She grasped her wrists and felt the rapid thud of her pulse.

Taking her time catching up with Mitch and Joey, Raine reminded herself of the promise she'd made to herself, telling herself a man with a small son would have needs, needs she couldn't fill. The knowledge twisted deep inside her, making Raine wonder if she'd ever truly find what she was searching for, if life would ever allow her to experience real freedom.

They walked to the play area, where Joey climbed into the sandbox and promptly began to dig. Tanner plopped down in the shade, gnawing on a piece of wood he'd found, and Raine lowered herself to a nearby bench. After a while, Mitch left Joey to his sand and joined her on the bench where he regarded her thoughtfully, his eyes drooping at the corners, matching the edges of his lips.

Raine looked at Joey, and, keeping her voice low, murmured, "This is the *new beginning* we drank to Saturday night?"

Mitch nodded, wondering if he'd always remember Saturday as the day his life changed. Had it really been only four days ago? The hand he pressed over his mouth did little to conceal a huge yawn.

"Joey's not a good sleeper?" she asked.

He settled his shoulders more comfortably along the back of the bench, stretching his legs out in front of him. "It's too soon to tell, isn't it?"

"What do you mean?" she asked, hiding a yawn of her own.

Mitch had a sudden image of some man keeping her awake until the wee hours of the morning. They'd both toasted to new beginnings. And while Joey was Mitch's, he wondered what Raine's new beginning was.

"I'll tell you why I'm tired if you'll tell me why you are," he said.

"I thought that was *I'll show you mine if you show me yours.*"

"All right."

She looked into his eyes and struggled with the implication of his words. Not more than a minute ago a hundred questions had zinged through her mind, and here she was wondering what he'd show her, what he'd like to see in return. Her thoughts spun whenever he was near. For heaven's sake, he said he'd never been married. So what was he doing with this child, this sweet, frightened, adorable child?

Mitch watched her wrestle with her emotions. Her foot began to jiggle, and he hid a secret smile. Of course she was curious about Joey, but her curiosity wasn't all he'd aroused. God, she was gorgeous. She was also a natural with kids. She'd opened her arms to Joey when he'd been frightened by Tanner, treating him with warmth and tenderness. He'd heard kids had pretty good instincts, and silently commended Joey on his choice of women to trust.

He'd felt a compelling attraction the first moment he'd looked into Raine's eyes. That attraction hadn't diminished, despite Joey's presence in his life. "The other night, you told me you're a great listener. Tell me, Raine, do men make a habit of telling you their problems?"

Raine shaded her eyes with her hand, silently searching his face. Slowly, her gaze slid away, to a place far in the distance. "I guess you could say that," she answered. "I must have one of those faces, you know, the kind that reminds everyone of their best friend, because more often than not, I find myself listening to people's troubles. Men talk to me about their girlfriends or pending divorces. Women tell me about their husbands and kids. Even my neighbor's cat comes to me when he's been yelled at for chasing birds."

Mitch watched her expression as she spoke, watched her shoulders slump a little more with every word. "And who do you tell your troubles to?" he whispered.

Her gaze swung to his, surprise in her voice and in her eyes. "Who, me? I don't have any troubles."

Oh yes she did, Mitch thought to himself. There was something in her eyes, like wistfulness, something in her smile, like hope, that made him think she'd lived through her share of hard times. He wanted to kiss her, here in the middle of the park. He toyed with the idea of doing just that, and it surprised him. He usually preferred to kiss a woman in more out-of-the-way places.

"What?" she asked.

Realizing he'd been staring, Mitch tilted his head to one side and murmured, "I was just thinking. You've met *my* new beginning. Tell me, Raine, what's yours?"

Her voice started out quiet, growing in intensity as she explained, "Saturday night was truly a fresh start for me. For the first time in my life, I'm really free to do as I like, to live for myself. For the first time in my life, I feel almost young, carefree."

"Are you newly divorced?" he asked.

She closed her eyes, and shook her head, making Mitch wonder what she was reliving. He had a feeling there was more to her new beginning than she'd told him, a lot more.

Before he could ask why she was suddenly free, she changed the subject and asked, "Why did you say it's too soon to tell if Joey's a good sleeper?"

"Last night was our first night together."

"You didn't have visitation rights until now?"

"Until last weekend, I didn't know I had a son, let alone the right to visit him." Mitch went on to tell her about the letter he'd received on Saturday, about Elizabeth Russell's will and his trip to Arizona to meet his son. She cast him a sympathetic look when he told her how Joey had screamed each time he, Taylor and Kyle had come anywhere near. She didn't interrupt or make any comment, and he understood why people went to her with their troubles.

She'd said she felt young and carefree for the first time in her life. He closed his eyes as his stomach knotted, desire warring with integrity. He wanted to kiss her. If they'd met two weeks earlier, he would have. Then, if she'd have told him she wanted to be carefree, he'd have said great, let's be carefree together.

Childish laughter drew both their gazes. Joey threw sand into the air and giggled as it sifted back down. Mitch realized he couldn't act on impulse anymore. Joey was his responsibility now, and all of his actions would evermore affect his son's life.

Moving back to his portion of the bench, he said, "This is the first time I've seen him play. I almost hate to make him stop. But how am I going to get that sand out of his hair?"

She folded her arms across her chest and smiled in Joey's direction. "He's definitely going to need a bath when he gets home."

"A bath?"

Raine laughed, as much from the way his voice cracked as from the expression on his face. She jumped to her feet, the wind blowing her short hair across her forehead. "Tell you what. I rode my bike here, and I'll trade you a ride home for a lesson in bathing a slippery two-year-old."

He stood, and her gaze followed him up. He took her hand in his, the gentle massage of his fingers sending warmth all over her body. "You'd better call Tanner if we're going to get Joey bathed before bedtime."

Mitch called his pet, and Tanner raced toward them, his long ears flying, a stick clamped between his teeth. When the dog reached them, he playfully circled twice, dropping the stick at Mitch's feet.

Joey took one look at the dog and again dived into Raine's arms. She looked from Mitch to Joey to Tanner, trying to decide who she felt the sorriest for.

Tanner, who whined in confusion.

Joey, who was terrified of his new life.

Or Mitch.

Tilting her head, she looked into Mitch's eyes, and it was all she could do to pull her gaze away. She'd known there was a strong passion inside her, and Mitch was certainly bringing that passion to life. But she'd only recently begun to recognize her own needs, and she didn't want to lose sight of them. She'd be wise not to give in to this particular passion. She'd be wise to let Mitch and Joey walk out of her life. For good.

She'd just take them back to her house, and she'd show Mitch how to bathe his son. When she'd finished, she'd let them walk away, and she'd be free. If she were wise, that's exactly what she would do.

Chapter Two

Raine led the way across her tiny patch of grass and up the back steps into her narrow home. Yes, letting Mitch walk out of her life would definitely be the wise thing to do. The problem was, when someone was in need, in genuine need, being wise wasn't always that simple.

"Lots of stairs," Joey proclaimed from the crook of Mitch's arm.

"Yes, Joey," she replied. "I have three floors. Can you hold up three fingers?"

Mitch was amazed when Joey held up his pointer fingers on both hands. What amazed him even more was the ease with which Raine handled him. "That's close," she murmured, pressing his thumb and little finger down. "See? One, two, three."

"One, two, three."

"Bring him this way, Mitch."

He followed, but then, with that walk, he'd have followed her anywhere. She had a great stride, a delectable sway with just the right amount of jiggle. If her body looked this good through navy blue shorts... He clamped his mouth shut and fixed his eyes elsewhere. Thoughts like these could make the next half hour or so extremely uncomfortable.

Mitch had been surprised when she'd suggested showing him how to bathe Joey here, in her house. He had a feeling there was a reason, he just didn't know what it could be.

Raine darted ahead of him through the kitchen, not stopping until they were all in the narrow bathroom. She instructed him to undress Joey while she turned on the faucet and took out a towel, shampoo and washcloth.

Joey had seemed so afraid of everything else, Mitch expected him to be terrified of the tub, too. Instead, the little boy took to the water like a seal, splashing and playing to his heart's content. Mitch was amazed, and mortified. He was a dentist, for heaven's sake, his fingers normally agile and adept when using intricate instruments in small spaces. But, with a soapy washcloth in one hand and a slippery toddler in the other, he felt more like a clumsy giant. By the time he was through, all three of them were soaked.

Joey wanted to play, and Mitch settled back, his knees on the floor, his forearms resting on the edge of the tub, his gaze trained on Raine. She laughed down at Joey, and Mitch swallowed the tightness in his throat. Drops of water clung to her cheeks, dampened tendrils of hair grazed her ear. Water splashed to one shoulder, and before his eyes, her white top seemed to disappear. The ridge of her collarbone shone through, and Mitch wished the water had landed lower.

He forced himself to look away, and swallowed an oath. Next, he'd be trying to cop a feel. He hadn't thought in such terms since college. Were all three Harris brothers destined to be juvenile forever? No. He wasn't eighteen, and a few touches would never be enough. At thirty-five, he wanted the whole picture, and he was beginning to think he'd met the woman he'd thought he'd never find.

Glancing at her again, Mitch saw Raine's lips raise to create enchanting dimples, then spread to reveal her even white teeth. His body reacted in a very primitive way. He barely knew her, certainly knew very little of her past. He remembered her face when she'd told him she was free, for the first time in her life. And though desire pulsed through his body, he knew he couldn't offer her any kind of freedom, not at this time in his life.

Raine laughed at Joey again, and glancing up at Mitch, felt her smile freeze on her face. He'd been watching her. That's all it took to set her pulse racing. She'd never met a man who could inspire such a reaction with only one look. His eyes were a dark shade of blue, his eyebrows a shade lighter than his hair, which was a little too long in the back to be considered conservative, and wavy enough to invoke heart-stirring thoughts. Everything about him evoked a subtle sensuality, but it was his mouth that repeatedly captured her attention, and her imagination.

Instead of letting her imagination run wild, she dodged the next set of splashes, averting his gaze at the same time. "That about covers Bathing 101." Rather than look at Mitch, she pressed the knob to drain the water while he wrapped Joey in a fluffy towel.

"I don't suppose you brought any clean clothes with you to the park?" she asked.

"Clean clothes?"

Raine smiled at the sheepish look on his face. Laying her hand on his arm, she murmured, "Don't worry, Mitch. You're still new at this. In a few weeks, it'll all be as natural to you as breathing."

She raised her eyes and gave him an exaggerated wink before handing him the disposable diaper he'd removed from Joey earlier. "This feels pretty light," she said. "It'll do until you get him home."

He laid Joey on the floor and slid the diaper beneath him. Raine was mesmerized by the gentleness in those big hands and in the way the small boy stared at him the entire time it took to fasten the adhesive tabs.

Mitch lifted Joey and murmured, "His grandmother said he was out of diapers, but with the trauma of Elizabeth's death and so many changes these past two weeks, he regressed."

Poor baby, Raine thought. Joey dropped his head to his father's shoulder, his eyes falling shut almost before he'd managed to pop his little thumb into his mouth.

"He's going to sleep," she whispered.

"Hallelujah."

Beneath the bright bathroom lights, Mitch's fatigue was clearly evident. Weariness showed around his eyes. Exhaustion pulled at the corners of his mouth.

"Mitch," she said softly, being careful not to disturb Joey. "Would you like something cold to drink?" At his nod, she led him from the bathroom and into the kitchen. Before peeking inside the refrigerator, she asked, "What would you like? A glass of iced tea? Can of soda?"

"Anything cold—"

"She didn't," Raine interrupted. "She did." Turning toward him, she said, "It looks like Holly and her friends wiped out the last of my beverages. All I have left is a half gallon of milk."

"Milk sounds great," he said.

"Really?" she asked, her eyes narrowing suspiciously.

"I'm a dentist. It's supposed to do a body good."

With her back to him, she took two glasses from the shelf and poured from the cardboard carton, thinking his body didn't need any more help to look good. "You're really a dentist?"

He nodded and accepted the glass from her hand. "Then I can't let Clay or Holly catch you here." At his raised eyebrow, she continued. "My brother and sister. They both go to college about a half hour away, though you'd never know they lived there, considering the amount of time they spend at my house. I've told them I'm going to have the time of my life, do all sorts of exciting things. If they find out I've invited a dentist inside, I'll never live it down."

"Dentists have a bad reputation."

"But Mitch, you're no ordinary dentist."

"No? Exactly what is an *ordinary* dentist?"

Settling her hands to the countertop, she looked him over. "Dentists usually come in two varieties. The first is on the small side, and quiet, usually wearing dark-rimmed glasses. They make me nervous."

"And the other variety?"

"The other type is big and gruff and looks as if he could yank a tooth out with his bare hands. They make me even more nervous."

"Do I make you nervous, Raine?"

She didn't answer, and his smile faded into another kind of look, unhurried and curious. He'd lowered his voice until it was smooth and deep and barely more than a whisper. It might have been because Joey was sleeping on his shoulder, but Raine didn't think so. She swore her blood suddenly felt like molasses, thick and heavy, and knew it had nothing to do with the fact that he was a dentist.

They sipped their milk in silence, both leaning against the counter. Mitch finally broke the stillness. "I've wondered what these places were like inside."

"I just moved in two weeks ago. The realtor called these old houses town houses. I prefer their original name, rowhouses. I mean, every house within the city limits is in town, right? These are all in a row, this one connected to the next, and so on. They're row houses."

"Makes perfect sense to me."

She cocked her head at him and, placing her glass on the counter, spun around, motioning for him to follow. "They have so much character. Come on. I'll give you a guided tour." Since he'd already seen most of the rooms downstairs, she gently took his arm and directed him up the narrow staircase, being careful not to wake Joey.

At the top of the stairs, she whispered, "This entire floor is the living area." She pointed to the new gray carpeting and sparse furniture. "On the third level is the bedroom and what was probably once the dressing room. I use it for storage. Do you know what I first fell in love with in this house?"

In the middle of a long swallow of milk, Mitch simply shook his head.

"The stairs. I just love having three separate floors."

Leave it to Raine to appreciate the one thing most people find fault with in this type of house. He was having a hard time resisting this bundle of restless energy. "Your home suits you."

Her eyes shone with the compliment. But Mitch believed it was true. Her home did suit her. It was unique, like her, small on the outside, and big on the inside. It had a character you couldn't quite see from the surface, with interesting nooks and nuances, and stairs that reached to places you could only imagine.

"My brother and sister don't agree. Even though they're both away at college, they would have preferred to have me stay where they left me."

"What about your parents?"

"They died," she said softly. "A little less than ten years ago. There were no relatives, and Mom and Dad had plenty of insurance, so the judge decided to let Holly and Clay stay with me."

Mitch caught the sadness in her voice. "You couldn't have been very old."

"I'd just turned nineteen. Holly was nine, and Clay was eleven."

He released a low whistle. "That's quite a responsibility for a nineteen-year-old." He had more relatives than he could count. They practically crawled out of the woodwork. If something had happened to his parents, he and his brothers would have been taken in, cared for. Even now, they wouldn't be forgotten.

"We're family. They needed me, and without my parents, they were all I had."

They'd needed her, but she'd only been nineteen. Mitch had been aware of an incredible attraction from the first moment he'd looked into Raine's eyes. Now, he was beginning to understand a few things about her, and worry narrowed his gaze.

"They needed you then," he said quietly. "What about your needs now?"

"We sold the big house to help pay for their educations. With my share, I bought this house. I'm adjusting to living on my own, and I'm taking flying lessons."

The worry in his eyes spread to the rest of him. She was free, and he wasn't.

He strode to the far wall and carefully laid Joey on the sofa. His son cuddled into a tight ball, and Mitch breathed a sigh of relief when he didn't wake up. Leaning over the coffee table, the only other piece of furniture in the room, he picked up a flight manual.

"Have you already started taking flying lessons?" Seeing the airplane on the manual's cover, actually holding the instructions in his hand, made what she'd just told him real. She really was going to soar. She really didn't want entanglements. He wondered if that was why she'd suggested bringing Joey here. Here, in her own home, she was in control. Here, she didn't feel tied down.

Mitch found himself gazing into her eyes, and the cadence of his breathing changed. She was so beautiful.

"Have dinner with me tomorrow."

She hesitated, and he had a feeling he wasn't going to like her answer. "Oh, Mitch. If we'd met a year from now, or in five or even ten years, I'd jump at the chance to see you. But now..." Her voice trailed off.

"Now you want your freedom." A clock chimed from a shadowy corner. Mitch cast a quick look at Joey to see if the chimes had startled him. The child slept on, and Mitch took a step toward Raine. "I wasn't thinking of locking you in my attic. I was only suggesting dinner." He swallowed against the vision of having Raine in his attic, of having Raine anywhere.

"Not only freedom, Mitch. I want excitement. I want to be wild!"

His eyes narrowed on her mouth, and he took another step closer. His voice dropped to a husky whisper. "You want wild? I'll show you wild." His hands slid to her waist, his arms drawing her close. He tilted his head, bringing his mouth down on hers.

They could have been standing on a cloud. They could have been anywhere in the world. Raine had never known milk to be an aphrodisiac, but the taste of Mitch's lips was wildly erotic. He moved his mouth over hers and stole her breath away. Every point of contact was explosive, his electric touch tingling over her entire body.

Mitch's kiss was like a discovery of something wonderful, exciting, enticing. Raine felt her body sway toward his, heard the deep breath he took and felt a yearning deep within her come to life. The kiss was gloriously sensuous, making her aware of his hand at her back, of the warmth filtering through her shirt and the desire building deep inside her.

Their lips parted slowly, and her eyes fluttered open. With her face only a few inches from his, she whispered, "That was definitely wild."

He smiled. He actually smiled. That smile of his made her heart turn over. It also made her nervous, as if he had something up his sleeve. Stepping out of his embrace, she murmured, "I have a class tomorrow night."

"Friday? Saturday?"

"Friday would be *fine.*" Raine grimaced at her choice of words, but it was that grimace that brought her back to reality. She hated the word *fine*. *Fine* was mediocre, not bad, ho-hum. *Fine* was boring, and she'd had enough of being boring to last a lifetime. Fine was something she'd have settled for before, before her new beginning. Now she wanted more. Now she wanted *wonderful*.

"What about Joey?"

Mitch felt her question siphon the blood from his face. She didn't seem to expect an answer, and as he reached for his son, he felt like a jerk. What kind of father was he? He'd only known he had a son for a few days, and he'd already completely forgotten him while kissing Raine. In his defense, he'd forgotten everyone else he'd ever known, as well. Hell, her kisses could make him forget his own name. But she hadn't forgotten. She was the one who wanted freedom and excitement, yet she was the one to remind *him* of his responsibility.

That kiss had wiped his mind clear of all but one thought. He wanted Raine McAlister. He wanted her in all the normal ways, wanted to kiss the smile from her lips, wanted to feel her rising passion. But she brought out other wants, as well, wants that had to do with more than simple desire, that had to do with forever, with a lasting relationship. Reality had dawned, and with that reality came the knowledge that she wanted freedom, a freedom she deserved.

He followed her down the stairs to the back door, where he heard Tanner's anxious barks. He strode down the steps, his arms filled with twenty-five pounds of sleeping child, his thoughts filled with regrets and self-recrimination.

Shushing Tanner, he opened the car door and coaxed the dog into the back seat. He somehow managed to slide Joey into his car seat without breaking either of the child's legs, which suddenly seemed three feet long and as fragile as uncooked spaghetti. He closed the passenger door as quietly as possible before walking around the car.

Raine had lowered herself to the second step, where she'd crossed her legs and was jiggling her foot. "I'll be surprised if he wakes up anytime soon," she said softly.

Mitch nodded, opened the car door and slid behind the wheel. He shut the door as gently as he could, lowered his window, then called, "Thanks for the bathing lesson."

"Anytime."

Without another word, he backed out of the driveway and pulled away into the late-summer night. *Anytime* she'd said, as if she fully expected him to call on her to help him again. The tone of her voice had been calmly accepting, but the way her foot jiggled was not.

She wanted independence. And he wanted her. How in the world could they both have what they wanted?

Each time Raine passed the laundry room, her gaze lingered on the freshly laundered, neatly folded shorts and T-shirt Mitch had left behind after Joey's bath the other night. Holly had stopped in, bringing her laundry with her. As usual, her younger sister had somehow managed to get out of doing her own laundry, and had stopped in later that night to pick up her clean clothes.

Mitch hadn't been back for Joey's things. She doubted he'd left them on purpose. After all, when it had come time to leave, he'd had his hands full with his child, and her mind had been full of reasons not to see him again, so that neither of them had remembered the clothes lying in a heap on her bathroom floor.

She'd expected him to call, or drop by. Certainly, by now he'd have missed the tiny tennis shoes Joey had worn that night. But he hadn't called, and by Saturday, Raine decided he didn't plan to. Why didn't he? He'd been thrust into fatherhood with very little preparation. She'd found his ineptitude at bathing Joey both comical and endearing. If anyone needed help, Mitch Harris did. But he wasn't ask-

ing for help. He wasn't asking for anything. Not even his
son's clothing and shoes.

Mitch was fun, wild and he could kiss like a dream. The
fact that he had a young son didn't detract from that wildness. His kiss had been a purely sensual experience. Her
body grew heavy and warm at the memory alone. She'd reacted to his kiss, and something warmed deep in her belly as
she remembered his reaction, remembered how he hard-
ened against her.

She closed her eyes, her hand fluttering down to the soft
purple shirt lying on her washer. She imagined Mitch's baf-
flement when he couldn't locate these blasted shoes. Maybe
he wasn't asking for her help, but that didn't mean she
couldn't offer.

An hour later she stood on his front step, Joey's clothes
tucked beneath her arm. She'd found Mitch's address in the
phone book, and the house, tucked into a quiet residential
area, hadn't been difficult to locate. Saturday-morning
cartoons blasted through the open living-room window, and
Tanner's barks sounded from the backyard. Raine pressed
the doorbell again, wondering what was taking so long.

The first thing she saw when the door opened a crack was
a chubby bare foot. "Hi, Joey," she smiled. The door
opened farther, and she found her gaze at knee level with a
pair of long, jean-clad legs. In the time it took to blink her
eyes, her gaze had followed those legs upward.

Mitch's jeans looked as if they'd been washed a hundred
times, the knees and fly faded to almost white. He wore no
belt, and a navy T-shirt was tucked into the waistband, fitting his chest and shoulders like a second skin.

By the time her eyes met his, all she could think to say
was, "I thought Joey might want his shoes."

For once, Mitch thought being slightly absentminded
might have proven to be an asset. He hadn't forgotten Joey's
clothes on purpose, but if he had, the plan would have bordered on brilliant.

Without releasing Joey's hand, he took a step back and gallantly gestured Raine inside. "Sorry I took so long to answer the door. I'm finding it's best not to turn my back on this little guy."

She found herself smiling in spite of herself, and took a step toward him. "You're learning."

"I'm a quick study." He took Joey's clothes and shoes from her and said, "Thanks, Raine, but you didn't have to bring these over. I would have gotten around to it before the snow flies."

"It's no trouble." Leaning down to Joey, she said, "Do you like cartoons?"

The two-year-old assumed a Ninja stance and, with a rather uncoordinated high kick, replied, "Turtle power!" The child quickly forgot her as he became engrossed in a cereal advertisement on television.

She straightened and met Mitch's gaze. "He seems to be adjusting quite well."

Mitch nodded. "He likes the new bed Taylor and Kyle and I put up, but isn't too sure about Taylor and Kyle. He's less leery of Tanner, but hasn't brought himself to touch him. He likes jelly sandwiches and hates peanut butter. I put away everything remotely harmful, from dish soap to pencils, although he did manage quite a mural on his bedroom wall before I thought about that one. This place is still a mess, but at least now it's safe."

She was laughing by the time he was through. "You've been busy."

Busy didn't begin to cover it. Upside down was more like it. But through it all, his thoughts had repeatedly returned to her. He remembered the way the breeze blew her hair across her temple, remembered the way she felt in his arms. He remembered her smile and the wistfulness in her eyes when she told him she wanted to be free.

Following the direction her gaze had taken, over the state of chaos his home was in, he murmured, "Half of me is looking forward to going back to work just to bring a level of normalcy to my life again, and the other half is worried about leaving Joey."

Joey chose that moment to dump out a plastic bucket of blocks, so Mitch didn't go on to tell her which part of him wanted her. The answer might have scared her away, because he wanted her in more ways than the obvious one. He wasn't quite sure how he was going to accomplish that. But there was one thing he *was* sure of. He wasn't going to give up.

"It looks like you're busy, and I should be going." She began edging toward the door.

Think fast, Harris. He had to come up with an excuse to get her to stay. "Actually, I'm not that busy." From her position in the living room, she eyed the dishes cluttering the kitchen counter and the toys strewn about practically every inch of floor. He had the grace to grin. "You offered me something cold to drink. Let me return the favor."

He led the way into the kitchen where he whisked some dry cereal from a chair and pulled it back for her. She sat down, and he strode to the refrigerator. "One week ago, this held two things. Beer and steak. Now there are hot dogs, apple juice, grapes and cheese. I'm afraid the only kind of soda I have is orange."

"Orange soda sounds *fine.*"

He wondered why she grimaced. "You're sure?" At her nod, he took two cans of orange soda from the refrigerator door and handed one to her.

"Me want soda, too."

Mitch looked from Joey to the microwave clock. It was awfully close to lunchtime, and the soft drink would spoil Joey's appetite, which wasn't all that great to begin with. But if he brought this up, Raine would undoubtedly leave. With barely a moment's hesitation, he poured some of his soda into a small cup and handed it to his son, thinking, what the heck, he and Joey could eat a late lunch.

Raine rarely missed a thing, and she certainly hadn't missed Mitch's speculative glance at the clock or the ease with which he'd reached a decision. "You could give lessons on that."

"Lessons?" he asked.

Could he really be unaware of his laid-back charm? Dishes cluttered the counter and sink. Cereal literally crunched beneath his feet, yet he sat down across from her and casually sipped his drink, seemingly oblivious to the disarray.

"I gave you a lesson in bathing Joey. You could return the favor. Maybe call it Easygoing 202."

"All right."

She watched him take a long swallow from his can . He hadn't bothered with glasses and ice, and Raine realized his casual style was as natural to him as breathing.

"All right, what?"

He finished the drink before answering. "You said you wanted lessons in being carefree. Welcome to Easygoing 202."

"I was kidding."

"Were you?"

Joey's plastic cup hit the floor then bounced twice, spraying orange liquid in every direction. He took one look at Mitch, started to cry and made a nosedive for Raine's lap.

Raine automatically cuddled Joey, meeting Mitch's gaze over the toddler's blond head. She really had been kidding about the easygoing lessons, but laid-back or not, the man needed help. The fact that he hadn't asked for hers made no difference whatsoever.

"You've probably noticed I could use a few pointers on child care," Mitch said.

Looking at his cluttered home, at the dirty dishes, littered floors, and at the serious-eyed child on her lap, Raine answered, "I'd say what you need even more is a wife."

His silence drew her gaze. "Are you applying for the job?"

From his position on the floor where he'd been haphazardly wiping up spilled soda, Mitch saw the worry in her eyes, in the nervous way she began to jiggle her foot. He could have kicked himself for putting it there.

Heaven knew he needed help. Watching the way Raine smoothed Joey's hair from his forehead, he knew he wasn't the only one. Mitch wasn't actively seeking a wife, nor was he searching for a mother for Joey. But if he were, Raine would be a wonderful choice.

Joey chose that moment to slide from her lap, and Mitch scrambled to think of some way to keep from scaring Raine away. Watching his son run into the adjoining room, Mitch said, "I was kidding, too. I'm not really looking for a wife. What I could use is a boatload of child-care tips."

He was kidding. Of course he was kidding. Raine took a deep breath, wondering why in the world she'd overreacted. Looking around his kitchen again, she said, "Maybe you really do need a wife, Mitch. I'm not interested in being tied down right now, but I do know some single women. I could introduce you, if you'd like."

"You want to fix me up with your friends?"

She nodded. "We could trade. I'll give you tips on child care, maybe introduce you to a few single women, and you can show me how to relax."

"Even-steven?" Mitch wiped his palm along his jeans before extending his hand to hers.

Raine took a deep breath. Before she could analyze the warmth in Mitch's gaze, she accepted his handshake. "Even-steven. And Mitch...I like your style."

"And I like yours." The pressure of his hand on hers changed subtly. The warmth in his eyes didn't.

She hadn't realized she'd started to jiggle her foot again. But Mitch had. He circled her ankle with his hand and looked deep into her eyes. "Lesson number one. Easygoing people don't jiggle their feet."

She felt his handprint on her ankle long after he'd pulled his fingers away. "Okay," she replied, just barely managing to keep her foot from bouncing once more. "And Mitch, just to keep us even, have you found satisfactory day care for Joey yet?"

He shook his head, and she proceeded to tell him about a friend of hers who ran a day-care center near the Lehigh Mall. She wrote the name and phone number on a scrap of paper she found lying on the table while Mitch tossed a towel toward the sink. He shrugged when it missed, and Raine said, "One more thing. I'd check into hiring someone to help with your cleaning, while you're at it. I'm afraid this place would scare any prospective brides away, in spite of those broad shoulders and that sexy smile of yours."

At the incredulous look on his face, she began to laugh. But when his expression grew serious, her laughter trailed away.

"All right," he murmured. "And just to keep us even... I have my pilot's license, and have a friend who owns his own plane. Want to go up with me sometime?"

There were a lot of things she'd like to do with Mitch, a lot of things she didn't think would be wise to ponder. In the end, the anticipation of flying surpassed her concern over the way his expression had her pulse throbbing.

"Rory, my friend with the plane, owes me a favor. Wednesday at seven okay with you?" he asked.

"Seven o'clock will be *fine.*" In her befuddled state, she completely forgot to grimace.

Chapter Three

Mitch couldn't help it if he was smiling when he walked up to the front door of Raine's town house Wednesday evening. He liked the air of calm and self-confidence he felt, liked the fact that he'd be spending the evening with the woman who'd occupied most of his thoughts since the moment he'd looked into her eyes.

The door opened, and the smile disappeared from his face. A tall, shirtless *younger* man flung the door against the wall as he cast a "Come on in" over his shoulder. He didn't wait for Mitch to follow, just turned and headed in the opposite direction.

Mitch stood there on the front step, trying to make sense of the situation. Maybe he had the wrong house. He checked the number above the door knocker, and knew he was in the right place. Maybe it wasn't the right time. He glanced at his watch, and knew he was only twenty minutes late. Maybe he wasn't in the right mind.

He entered the kitchen in time to see Raine bite a piece of thread with her teeth then slip a shirt over the half-naked man standing before her. What was left of Mitch's earlier self-confidence slid completely away.

"Hi, Mitch," she called over her shoulder. "I'll be with you in a minute."

The young man winked at Mitch. "I'm Clay. You must be the guy who's taking Cloudie flying."

Mitch didn't like the sound of this, didn't like the fact that Raine had mentioned him to this young punk. The half-naked man pulled the shirt closed, focusing all his attention on the woman with her hands all over him. In a tone of voice Mitch didn't appreciate anyone *else* using on her, the other man whispered, "You look different, Raine."

"It's this hair of mine," Raine murmured with an affectionate smile that made Mitch more uneasy by the second. "Growing my hair out seemed like a good idea three months ago. Now I'm not so sure."

Mitch thought she looked great. The other man evidently did, too, because he leaned down to kiss her cheek, and it was all Mitch could do to keep from turning on his heel and hightailing it out of there.

"Thanks, Cloudie. Just one more thing. Could I borrow your car tonight?"

While Raine handed him her keys, Mitch wondered what he'd have walked in on if he hadn't arrived twenty minutes late. He fought the urge to punch the guy's face in. She'd said she wanted to be wild and free. Mitch hadn't expected her to mean this.

With a grin that looked vaguely familiar, a grin that went from boyish to that of a man, the other man murmured, "You're the best. I don't know what I'd do without you." With that, he sauntered out of the room, calling goodbye before the door had slammed shut behind him.

"I swear he's never learned to close a door properly," Raine declared with a shake of her head.

"You've known him a long time?"

"Longer than I care to admit. You've heard me mention Clay?"

"Vaguely." The name sounded familiar.

"He had a date tonight and asked me to sew on a button. You know how exasperating brothers can be."

Brothers? Of course. Clay. Her younger brother. Tension drained out of him like air whooshing from a balloon. No wonder Clay's smile had looked familiar, it reminded him of Raine's. It was probably a good thing Mitch hadn't punched his face in, after all.

They took Mitch's car to the private airstrip south of Allentown, Raine's excitement growing with every mile. She'd only been up in a plane twice, when she'd taken Clay and Holly to Walt Disney World years ago.

She and Mitch talked along the way, mostly about general topics, and about Joey. "There's no doubt that little boy is a Harris," Mitch declared. "He has a stubborn streak wider than he is tall."

"How does he like Tammy's day care?"

"He loves it. Said he played Ninja Turtles all day long today."

Mitch drove the way he did everything, as if he didn't have a care in the world. He strummed the fingers of his right hand against the armrest, curling the fingers of his other hand around the steering wheel. Watching him, Raine found herself looking forward to spending time with this man, this nonchalant come-what-may dentist who made no demands, who'd exchange lessons on child care for lessons on being carefree.

He pulled into the country airstrip, circled to the back of a hangar and put the car in park. Raine was out the door before he'd turned off the ignition. Moving to the airplane facing the runway a short distance away, she said, "He's a beauty."

"He?" Mitch asked.

"I always think of airplanes as masculine beings."

Mitch was suddenly there, his blue eyes full of life, and warmth, and an unhurried glint that made her wonder what he was thinking. He opened the airplane door, and Raine reached up, ready to pull herself up into the plane.

The sweater she'd draped over her shoulders slipped away. Mitch caught it with one hand. He brought his other hand up to cup her upper arm, stopping her movements. She swung her head around, glancing from Mitch's hand to his face, mere inches away.

With the pad of one finger, he grazed the thick, purple scar on her upper arm. "Raine, what happened?"

Mitch watched her scan the hand covering her arm, watched her bite her lower lip, as if trying to think of some way to minimize the incident. Mitch traced another path around the scar with his finger, gently, softly, waiting for her to explain.

"I had a little accident."

He looked into her eyes, and found hers serious. "Are you accident-prone?"

She shook her head. "Actually, this was my first. I'm never even sick. Holly's always caught colds, and Clay's the one with all the broken bones."

"And you've always taken care of them."

Mitch had a feeling she'd have started jiggling her foot if she'd been sitting. As it was, she worried her bottom lip, and tried to make light of the situation. "You make me sound like an old spinster sister."

He moved closer, his voice dropping to a whisper. "Believe me, that isn't the way I see you."

He touched the center of the scar. "I'm a doctor, and I know a serious injury when I see one. How did it happen, Raine?"

She was staring at his hand, but Mitch doubted it was what she was seeing. Her brown eyes were more serious than he'd ever seen them, and her voice, when it came, was so soft it seemed to come from a long way off.

"I was clipping the hedges at my old house about two months ago. I could hear children playing next door. Out of the corner of my eye, I saw their puppy run toward the busy street. Children's voices called to him, but the puppy didn't stop, and a little girl chased after him. I don't remember dropping the hedge trimmers, don't really even remember running after her. All I remember is the way her hair flew behind her as she chased her puppy, and the blare of horns and the screech of tires.

"I heard a scream. Later, they told me it was my own. Cars were swerving to miss the child, hitting other cars, instead. Glass was flying, and the little girl froze in fear. A truck was heading right for her. I grabbed her arm and jumped. I don't remember the rest."

"You saved the girl's life." Mitch lowered his head, his lips brushing her soft skin. God, she'd nearly been killed. He might have never known her. The thought sent a heaviness through him, the kind of heaviness you feel when something wonderful is over, never to be again.

"Maybe," she replied. "But if not for that little girl, I wouldn't be reaching for the sky right now. I could have died that day, without doing any of the things I've always dreamed of doing."

The first moment he'd looked into her eyes, he'd instinctively sensed she was an incredible woman. Now he knew his instincts had been correct. She didn't seem very comfortable talking about herself, but Mitch had a feeling she'd confided more than she normally did. And for some reason, he felt incredibly honored.

"Come on," he murmured. "You have a date to fly an airplane."

The seriousness slowly left her eyes, replaced by a gentle smile that nearly took Mitch's breath away. He helped her up into the plane, and strode around to the other side. It took several deep breaths to lift the heaviness from his stomach, and to chase from his mind the image of her running through traffic to save a child's life.

He was beginning to understand a few things about Raine McAlister. Her quest for freedom wasn't something frivolous. Neither was his admiration, or his growing feelings for her.

Seated in the plane, their seat belts fastened, he cast her what he'd been told was his most beguiling grin. "You want to have a good time? Well, hold on to your seat, I'm just the man to show you one."

Raine watched him flip switches and check gauges, her excitement building. When he started the engine, and the plane began to move forward over the runway, she laughed out loud. Moments later, they were airborne, Raine's stomach somewhere far below.

The plane climbed and banked and dipped, and Raine marveled at the view. "Look over there." She pointed into the distance where hills rolled into valleys, and valleys spread to the edge of mountains. "Isn't Pennsylvania incredible?"

His answer was a dip on the control, which sent the plane zooming down, Raine's laughter following close behind. "Are you sure you know how to fly this?" she called.

"I'm sure. Kyle, Taylor and I all learned five years ago. It was one of our many bets to outdo one another."

She watched him man the controls and had to admit he did look as if he knew what he was doing. His style was just so incredibly casual, it was impossible not to notice. The way he sat, for instance, with his head cocked to one side, his shoulders filling the width of the seat, his bent knees spread out. How could anyone be so relaxed?

She found herself staring at his mouth, his slow grin swirling over her like fog. From somewhere came the realization that he wasn't all easygoing charm. She glimpsed a wildness about him, subtle, subdued, half-hidden.

"Your brothers sound like daredevils. I have a feeling they aren't the only ones."

"I've had my share of excitement."

"Like what?"

"There was the time all three of us 'borrowed' Dad's new car and went cruising in Philadelphia to find girls and ended up lost, somewhere in Chinatown."

Raine smiled, unaware that she'd relaxed during his tale. The airplane soared through a cloud, but she wasn't watching the sky. She was watching Mitch. By the time he'd finished describing another adventure in which an overanxious father had chased him and his brothers through the crowded sidewalk cafés of Paris, demanding, in broken English, that they stay away from his daughters, her undiluted laughter was soaring on the evening breeze along with the plane.

The color of his eyes outshone the blueness of the sky, and she had a feeling Mitch knew it. "You call that nothing out of the ordinary? I'm the one who needs more excitement in my life."

"You're the one who saved a little girl's life." His words were casual enough, but his tone was deep with admiration, an admiration she wasn't entirely comfortable with.

Something about him was different, more so than any other man she'd ever met. That difference skirted the edges of her mind then thinned to transparency a moment before she figured it all out. Mitch Harris warmed her heart, and worried her at the same time.

"Okay," he said. "Your turn."

"My turn for what?"

"You said you wanted adventure. Do you want to fly this plane or don't you?"

This was not the time in her life to back away from challenges, no matter how small. Easing her hands to the control in front of her, she waited for his instructions.

"Grab that bar with both hands until you get the sense of how it feels. That's it. Hold it firmly. Now bring your hands down. Slow and easy."

Her scent, her nearness, stirred the heat in his veins, giving his words of instruction an entirely different meaning, so that they both turned their heads in the same instant. Mitch read an awakening yearning in her eyes, and he'd bet both his brothers it was due to more than the exhilaration of flying.

He instinctively pushed up on the control and the plane's small engine groaned as it began its climb. He watched her, and her gaze slid away, her concentration now fixed on controlling the plane, on holding the lever steady.

She'd tucked her hair behind her ear, exposing her profile. The line of her jaw looked smooth, her neck long and sleek. He wondered what her skin would feel like beneath his fingertips, beneath his lips, and desire curled deeper into his body.

Her hands squeezed the control in front of her, and he wanted to move them to his body. He saw a pulse beating in her throat, but instead of meeting his gaze, she lowered her chin and squared her shoulders.

"Do you think Joey would like to fly?" she asked.

Mitch shrugged, mumbling something vague, wondering if she was aware of what she'd just done, aware that she'd mentioned Joey, calling to mind the differences in their goals: he'd suddenly found himself with a child to raise; she'd raised two already, and now wanted no further commitments.

Mitch felt the change in her, and he didn't blame her. She had every right to her own goals. He just wanted to be part of them, that's all.

He kept the conversation light after that, explaining the laws of flight, showing her how to bank the plane, how to climb and how to soar. She listened intently, but she kept her eyes carefully averted from his, so he couldn't see the light in their depths, the light that drew him to her, that said she was drawn to him, too.

He brought the plane in low, then executed a perfect landing, aware the entire time that Raine had distanced herself from him. In more ways than one.

He taxied up the runway, trying to think of some way to keep from losing her. He'd shut off the engine and had opened the door, but was no closer to a plan than he'd been for the past hour.

Pointing the car toward Allentown a short time later, the conversation once again centered on Joey. "He's really adjusting okay?" she asked.

"He's a tough little guy. Joey's adjusting better than his grandmother, I'm afraid."

"You've spoken to her?"

"I called her last night. She's mourning Elizabeth, and misses Joey terribly."

"Tell me about Elizabeth," Raine whispered.

Mitch took his eyes from the road and looked deeply into hers. "There isn't much to tell. I met her at a dental convention in Phoenix over three years ago."

"She was a dentist?"

Remembering her description of dentists, Mitch almost laughed at her expression. "She was a dentist, in her late thirties."

"Does Joey look like her?"

Gazing into Raine's eyes, Mitch could barely remember what Elizabeth Russell had looked like. "No, Joey actually looks more like Taylor."

"So you and Elizabeth met at the convention."

"We both spent too much time at the punch bowl, and before we knew it, we were in her room. She told me she was on the Pill. I believed her."

"She tricked you?"

"Her mother, Eva, told me Elizabeth had always wanted a child. She didn't think of it as tricking me. She was just trying to achieve something she'd always dreamed of having. Anyway, the next morning each of us had a hangover. She went back to Tucson and I came back to Allentown. I never heard another word from her, until I received the letter from her attorney.''

"And now you have Joey."

"And now I have Joey. And do you know what, Raine? I'm glad."

They drove on in silence, until Raine said, "I was young when my parents died, and I know a lot of people wouldn't have wanted the responsibility of raising a nine- and eleven-year-old brother and sister. They're all the family I have, and looking back, I wouldn't change a thing, either. They're worth everything I had to give up. But it's funny how much easier you've adjusted to Joey than I did to having full responsibility of Holly and Clay. You obviously take things in your stride a lot easier than I do."

There was nothing *funny* about the way he felt when he was with Raine. If he'd adjusted to Joey more easily than she had to her brother and sister, it probably had a lot to do with how young she'd been at the time, and that she'd lost both her parents. He was thirty-five years old. Elizabeth's death had been startling, but he'd never loved her, just as she'd never loved him.

He gazed into Raine's eyes with what he'd been told was his best trust-me expression. "You need to spend more time with me," he murmured. "I'll show you the ropes and have you loosened up in no time."

"That's what I'm afraid of."

Mitch noticed she was biting her bottom lip, and had to give her credit. Not one double entendre escaped her. "Want to hear something interesting?"

"What?" she asked.

"You and Joey's grandmother think alike. She said I should look for a wife, too. You told me you had a couple of friends who are single. Any of them good with kids?"

"Let me think...."

It was all Mitch could do not to grin. *Harris, you are a genius.* He'd wondered how in the world he could put her at ease, yet continue to see her at the same time, and it had been a snap. As easy as one, two, three.

It took a few seconds to realize the repetitious movement visible from the corner of his eye was the jiggling of one sneaker-clad foot. He regarded the fidgety woman seated next to him. On second thought, maybe this wasn't going to be as easy as he'd thought.

From his office doorway, Mitch watched his brother in action. Kyle sat in Mitch's office chair, his feet on the desk, while the receptionist attempted to straighten the clutter around him.

"Perhaps you'd be more comfortable in the outer waiting area," Candace said, pushing Kyle's feet to the floor before dropping several pens and pencils into the desk drawer.

Kyle's shoes hit the floor at the same time Candace shoved the drawer closed. With a twinkle in his eye, he winked at Mitch and made a production out of ogling the no-nonsense receptionist. With what Mitch had come to recognize as his brother's most infuriating tone of voice, Kyle declared, "I prefer the view from right here, Candy."

The receptionist straightened, bristling over Kyle's tone and his choice of nickname. With teeth practically gnashing, she walked past Mitch. "Your brother is the most... Good night, Doctor, I'll see you in the morning."

"Goodbye, Candace."

"Bye, Candy," Kyle called.

Candace stormed through the door, and Mitch knew she would have slammed it shut with enough force to rattle its hinges, if not for the automatic return.

"Your receptionist could be quite a looker. Too bad she's so disciplined."

"What are you doing here, Kyle? I thought my office made you nervous."

"It does, but needling Candy makes up for it."

"One of these days she's going to get even with you," Mitch replied, sauntering into the room.

"I'm looking forward to it. Want to grab a burger with me?" Kyle asked.

Mitch eyed his older brother. Kyle made no bones about his feelings regarding Mitch's office. He swore he didn't like the smell of it or the sounds that emanated from it. He claimed the pointed instruments had been invented with the sole purpose of scaring the living daylights out of people like him, and the reclining chairs resembled those used in torture chambers in old horror flicks. The only time he came here was when he had something on his mind, something important.

"Let's go back to my place," Mitch said. "I'll pick Joey up and we can throw some steaks on the grill."

An hour later, their plates were stacked in the sink in Mitch's small kitchen. The brothers sat on the deck, each gripping a cold can. From down the street they heard laughter. A cicada hummed from a tree out front and Joey played with a new truck at their feet.

So far, Mitch had no idea what was bothering Kyle. His attempts at conversation had ended with grunts and mumbled phrases. Mitch decided to wait it out. If Kyle wanted to say something, eventually he'd say it.

"Who would have believed you'd end up like this." Kyle gestured to the deck, the quiet subdivision, the typical three-bedroom house. "We used to be so wild. Now look at you. You're a dentist, and you have a kid."

Joey chose that moment to look up from his toy. He warily eyed his Uncle Kyle, then his father. Mitch winked and grinned at him, and was rewarded with a shy smile. That little smile did things to Mitch, puffed and pulled at his insides. It made him feel like a giant, sturdy and strong, and as fragile as blown glass.

"Taylor called. He isn't much better."

Now Mitch knew they were about to get to the bottom of what was bothering Kyle. "What did Taylor want?"

"He's taking this bet of ours much too seriously."

So that's what was bothering Kyle. The standing bet they'd had since they were kids. "You just don't want to give up the trophy," Mitch returned. "What's Taylor doing that's so serious?"

"He's seeing a leggy brunette with three kids. Three, for heaven's sake! First you, and now him. It would be just like Taylor to show up at the folks' party this fall with not only a woman on his arm, but with a vanful of kids trailing after him."

"Taylor didn't mention any woman when he was here the other day," Mitch said.

Kyle finished the last swallow from the can in his hand and let the front legs of his chair touch the floor. "Well, that's all he talked about last night. How about you? Any good prospects?"

The image of short blond hair, dark brown eyes and a body to lose yourself in wound its way through Mitch's mind. The Harris brothers had always shared their latest dating status with one another, but Mitch wasn't ready to tell his brother about Raine.

"You make getting married sound like buying real estate or securing a better job."

"You don't have anyone in mind, either?" Kyle asked.

"Either? Don't tell me Sexy-voice-Harris, the guy who has women swooning at his feet, can't get a date!"

Kyle started to swear, but because of Joey, stopped himself in the nick of time. Mitch laughed, the bout failing to ease the pressure he'd felt in his chest since the last time he saw Raine. There was more to the pressure than suddenly finding himself responsible for a two-year-old. This pressure had to do with wanting the love of a beautiful woman, one who just happened to want her independence.

Carrying Joey in his arms, Mitch walked down the steps with Kyle, past the basketball hoop and beyond, until they came to the red sports car parked along the street. Once inside the vehicle, Kyle poked his head through the open window, and said, "Finding the perfect woman isn't easy, is it, Mitch?"

Shaking his head, Mitch suddenly felt restless. Kyle was looking for a perfect woman, but his brother would be better off searching for the *right* woman.

Mitch had a feeling he'd already met the right woman. But he had a problem. His *right woman* wasn't looking for a perfect man. She wasn't even looking for a relationship. And dammit, he'd found one.

Kyle squealed away from the curb, and Mitch wished he'd challenged his brother to a game of one-on-one. Instead, he climbed the stairs and he and Joey went inside. He had to make some phone calls. He had to find a baby-sitter for Joey, and come up with a foolproof plan to show Raine that she didn't really need her freedom. He had to convince her that what she really needed was him.

Raine pulled into her driveway to find Mitch lounging on her back steps. Blowing a strand of hair from her eyes, she thought there ought to be a law against anyone being *that* relaxed.

Parking her car in the garage, she opened her door and pulled two sacks of groceries into her arms. She hadn't seen Mitch since they'd flown in the airplane, and she'd tried to tell herself she hadn't thought of him every day since.

"Hello."

Her steps slowed in response to his smooth, low voice. "Hi, Mitch."

"Long day?"

She nodded, and stepped up to the first step.

Mitch stretched his long legs out then stood. "Me, too."

He wore navy Dockers, a sky-blue shirt, the sleeves rolled up past his wrists, and a red paisley tie. Maybe he'd had a long day, but it didn't show on his face, in his posture. He took one sack of groceries from her, making a show of staggering beneath its weight. "What's in here? A ton of bricks?"

"Close." With her free hand, she unlocked the door then led the way toward the kitchen. "Where's Joey?"

"With my parents."

Mitch placed his sack next to hers, and leaned one hip against the counter where she'd piled her purse, her flight manual and the other sack of groceries.

"I went directly from work to the airport, and directly from the airport to the grocery store."

"Another flying lesson?"

Raine nodded. "The film we watched today gave me butterflies. Being your copilot was great, but I can't wait to experience the real thing, fly a plane myself." She began taking articles from the bags, darting to the cupboards and refrigerator and back again while she talked.

Mitch handed her the items from one sack, a grin stretching his lips. "What are you looking at?" she asked suspiciously.

His gaze homed in on her mouth. "You," he murmured. "I'm looking at you, and wondering..." He leaned closer, and instead of finishing his statement, he briefly touched his lips to hers.

She stepped away from him and reached for another carton. "Mitch..."

"What is all this?" he asked, holding up a small square cardboard box, and changing the subject at the same time.

"This is my dinner, which, by the way, I missed tonight."

"You actually *eat* this stuff?" He flipped through the cartons, holding up several at a time. "Microwave lasagna.

Microwave almond chicken.'' He swallowed dramatically. ''Microwave meat loaf. Now there's a treat.''

Raine started to laugh. It began as a small sound at the back of her throat and gradually built, floating up from someplace deep inside her. With the laughter, her fatigue eased.

For a long moment, she looked at him. There was no doubt about it. He had a way of relaxing her. She wasn't sure how he did it. She wasn't sure she wanted to find out, but there was one thing she *was* sure of. Something warm settled in her heart each time she saw him. Something warm and smooth and exciting.

''I'm starved,'' he said, his voice dropping low.

''Which would you prefer? The meat loaf or the lasagna?''

''Pizza.''

''I don't have pizza.''

''Good. Let's find a pizza place where we can sink our teeth into a piping-hot pizza loaded with thick, melting cheese and sausage.''

Raine contemplated his suggestion. Neither the meat loaf nor the lasagna looked very appetizing at the moment. ''Just give me a minute to put the rest of these groceries away.''

''Leave 'em.''

''What?''

''Leave them. They'll still be here when you get back.''

Raine looked at the clutter on her counter, and Mitch said, ''Easygoing people don't worry about a little clutter.''

After a moment, she murmured, ''Let's compromise. I'll put away all the cold stuff and—'' she gulped ''—leave the rest for later.''

For the first time in her life, Raine left her house with the kitchen a mess. She felt an odd sense of satisfaction in that feat. That satisfaction flitted around in her empty stomach while she darted ahead of Mitch to his car. ''Let's hurry, Mitch. This easygoing person is starving!''

A short time later, when the waitress put the pan of piping-hot pizza on the table between them, Raine and Mitch both moaned out loud. Neither talked as they each scooped up a large slice, the melted cheese stretching from the pan to their plates. They were both well into their second slices before either said an intelligible word.

"What do your parents think of Joey?"

"You wouldn't believe the fuss! You'd think nobody ever had a grandchild before."

"Few people learn of a grandchild the way your parents learned about Joey."

Mitch's voice grew serious. "They love him, and they can't get over how much he looks like I used to as a kid."

His throat tightened at the understanding in her eyes. He'd promised himself he wouldn't place any demands on her, on her time, certainly not on her emotions. It was going to be hard to live up to that promise.

Raine raised a slice of pizza and said, "This is definitely better than microwave meat loaf."

"Why do you eat those dinners?"

She shrugged. "They're easy. They're nutritious. When Clay and Holly lived with me, I prepared nutritious home-cooked dinners. I don't want to go through all the fuss anymore."

Her statement told him more than he wanted to know. Each time he saw her, he wanted to see her more. And each time, he better understood her reasons for not wanting to be tied down. "What else did you learn in flight class this afternoon?" he said, changing the subject.

"As I told you before, we watched a film, then talked about air speed and wingspans, that sort of thing."

Mitch thought about the risks involved in flying a one-engine airplane, and remembered the risk she'd already taken with her own life when she'd saved that little girl's life a couple of months ago. A knot formed in his stomach. He didn't want to lose her, didn't want her to take unnecessary risks. "Doesn't it bother you to think about flying, more specifically, to think about crashing?"

"Did it bother you?"

Mitch swallowed a gulp of soda instead of answering. She had him there.

"Besides," she continued, "heights don't scare me." She said it with such clarity, such vehemence, it had to be true.

"Why flying? There are hundreds of ways to take chances. Drive a race car. Walk a tightrope. Why did you choose flying?"

"I'm not sure. But even when I was little, I always climbed the tallest trees." Her pizza was momentarily forgotten, her fatigue merely a memory. "I think I chose flying because of the view. My favorite place in the entire world is in the Pocono Mountains. There's an old lookout up there that's like a watchtower to the whole county. You can practically see forever. It takes your breath away."

Gazing across the small table at Mitch, Raine knew the view from the Pocono Mountains wasn't the only thing that took her breath away. For the briefest moment, she wished she would have met him a year from now. Wished this was the right time in her life for a relationship. Wished he'd stop looking at her like that. Wished he'd keep looking at her that way forever.

But this wasn't the right time in her life for such wishes. And she'd promised herself no ties. *Promised.* She'd given up her dream of learning to fly ten years ago to raise Holly and Clay. She couldn't give it up again, not when she was so close.

Breaking their eye contact, she watched as Mitch scooped up another piece of pizza. Her gaze settled on his hands. "I thought dentists' hands were supposed to be soft and pale."

Mitch lifted his hands, turning them, inspecting the callouses and bony knuckles. "Another dentist myth shot to hell."

She couldn't help but laugh at his expression. "What about you?" she asked. "There are hundreds of occupations you could have chosen. Why did you choose to become a dentist?"

"I didn't have any cavities when I was a kid. I loved going to the dentist."

"You're kidding! Nobody *loves* going to the dentist."

"Thanks. You're working wonders with my ego."

"You're welcome. Go on."

"It fascinated me. The human mouth still fascinates me. Did you know that your tongue is more sensitive than any other part of your entire body?"

Raine's tongue slowly stroked the inside of her mouth, between her teeth and over her lips. "More sensitive than *any* other part?" she said hoarsely.

She couldn't control the way her voice had deepened, the way her eyelids had lowered, the way her heart seemed to stop. She couldn't control the look she read in Mitch's deep blue eyes, or the way that look made her feel.

"We could try to prove the textbooks wrong." His words were teasing, but his voice was whisper-deep, sensuously intense. It was obvious he was thinking of other sensitive body parts. His or hers, she couldn't tell.

Raine wasn't the blushing type, but a warm, rosy glow tinged her cheeks. And her cheeks weren't the only places she felt warm. Searching for a new topic, she said, "So, you're one of those lucky people who love what they do for a living."

"Don't you?" His voice was still deep, but he seemed to be trying to help her move this conversation to safer ground.

"Don't I what? Love what I do for a living? It pays the bills."

"Why did you choose it if it's so terrible?"

"I didn't say it was terrible. It's just an office job."

"Been there long?"

"Almost ten years. Since shortly after my parents' accident. You say I'm fidgety?"

He hadn't said it lately.

"Well, after sitting behind a desk all day, I have to be."

"Fidgety?"

Raine could tell he wasn't following her thought processes. "I used to waitress at the airport restaurant. I loved that job, but what I wanted to do even more was become a flight attendant. I'd signed up for some training, and for flying lessons. But when my parents died, I had to quit."

"Why?" Mitch asked.

"The office job has better benefits, a great insurance plan, retirement packages. After my parents' accident, I had to consider those things. Clay and Holly needed security. We all did."

"And now?"

"Now, it's time to go." Raine pushed herself from the table. She didn't want to talk about what she needed now, how the look in Mitch's eyes made her yearn for more than just a look. She'd take her new life one step at a time. But sometimes that one step felt more like a flying leap.

They were both quiet as they drove from the restaurant. She didn't understand his silence. Now that she thought about it, she realized he always grew quiet when she talked about what she wanted in life.

Worry enveloped her as he parked in front of her house. She couldn't let Mitch influence her. She needed to do what she wanted now that Clay and Holly were grown.

What she wanted.

How she wanted.

When she wanted.

She couldn't let others' expectations keep her from her dreams. Not even blue-eyed men with rugged hands and slow steady smiles.

"Raine, I want to—"

Before he could finish, she interrupted. "You know, Mitch, I do have one friend who might be perfect for you. She's newly divorced, but she says she loves kids. Do you want me to see if I can set up a meeting?"

"A meeting?" he asked skeptically.

"Unless you aren't serious about finding a wife."

He gazed out the windshield for a full ten seconds before answering. Without looking at her, he watched a cat stretch on her front step, and said, "Oh, I'm serious about finding a wife, Raine. Very serious."

She pushed open the car door. "Great. I'll see what I can put together."

"All right. Let me know what you come up with."

"I will," she answered. "I'll call you as soon as I talk to my friend."

"Okay."

Stepping from the car, she said, "The pizza was great. It was truly better than microwave meat loaf." Her voice quivered and her hand trembled.

"Good night, Raine," he whispered, his voice fading away on her name.

She hurried up the short sidewalk and opened her front door. Without turning around, she closed it, thinking that if she wasn't careful, she'd fall for Mitch. And falling for Mitch Harris would definitely be classified as taking a flying leap.

Chapter Four

"Hello. I was about to give up, but I thought, I've already let it ring fourteen times, what's one more?" Mitch's voice came through the phone line that Raine had just run inside to answer.

Panting a bit from her unexpected dash, she took a deep breath before replying. "I was down the street, feeding my neighbor's cats."

"You were feeding cats in the street?"

"Are you trying to start something?"

"I wouldn't touch that one."

His innuendo made her smile. She'd told herself a hundred times she wasn't becoming involved with Mitch, she wasn't giving in to his attraction. She'd offer him friendship, and introduce him to a few of her single friends. She'd told herself a hundred times she wasn't about to take a flying leap.

No matter what she'd told herself, that smooth voice of his sifted through her resolve and gave her airy hopes of letting go. It made her think she might even survive a flying leap.

"Rule number two. Easygoing people don't feed their neighbor's cats!"

"I couldn't just let them starve," she declared.

"Of course you couldn't."

"How did your date with Larielle go?" Raine asked, straining for a neutral topic and still trying to calm her heartbeat down.

"That depends. Just how close of a friend is Larielle?"

"Why?" she asked.

"Because, after tonight, she may not like you."

"What happened?"

"Well," Mitch began, "dinner was okay, or at least the food was. Larielle seemed more intent on devouring me."

"You didn't find her attractive?"

"It was impossible to tell. Her hair was three colors of red, her nails too long to be real. Nobody has aqua eyes without a little help, and I couldn't actually see her face through her makeup."

Raine was laughing out loud before Mitch was through, and that worried her. The way Mitch made her feel worried her. The way his gaze rested on her whenever they were together, like a moonbeam on a darkened river. The way his voice dipped low and suggestive, like a whisper echoing through a deep valley. The way he stood, the way he sat, the way he moved, lazily, as if what he was doing at that particular moment was the only thing on his mind. She wondered if he'd make love the same way, as if he had all the time in the world, and felt sad that she'd never know.

She really doubted Mitch knew what he did to her, and where he took her imagination. His drawl was too laid-back to be fake, his smile too slow to be practiced. It was as if he really didn't have a care in the world.

Raine realized he was still talking about his evening with Larielle Lewis, and she felt compelled to point out a few facts about her friend. "She really is a nice person. I wouldn't have suggested you take her out if I didn't think so."

"I believe you."

"So you won't be asking her out again?"

"No." Mitch didn't tell Raine the true reason he wouldn't be asking Larielle out a second time. It didn't really have anything to do with her hair color or her fingernails, although he did prefer women who were a little less brash. Larielle was nice enough, and interested enough, and eager enough. She simply wasn't Raine.

"I have a few more single friends. I'll see what I can do."

"You do that," he murmured. "Between you, my brothers and the rest of my relatives, I'll be married in no time."

"Your family is trying to fix you up, too?"

"Even before Joey, my relatives considered Taylor, Kyle and I over the hill. They're afraid that if they don't find us wives soon, we'll go to our graves as crotchety old bachelors."

As always, his portrayal of his family had her laughing out loud. "Now that your parents are back, you probably won't be needing my advice on child care."

"My mother is a great cook, and an immaculate housekeeper. But when I asked her about getting stains out of Joey's white pants, she told me not to bother with the knees, said he'd probably be getting more stains on them, anyway."

It was obvious Mitch had come by his relaxed personality naturally. "Try making a paste of liquid laundry detergent, a heavy-duty presoak and a little powdered dishwasher detergent, then pour it right on the stain. It works great on white clothes. At least it always worked on Holly's and Clay's."

"Thanks, Raine, but that really wasn't the reason I called."

"It wasn't?"

"Do you like football?"

"Clay played in high school." She answered automatically, cradling the phone to her ear so both hands were free.

"But do you like it?"

"Yes, I guess I do. Why?" She rinsed her coffee mug then tipped it upside down to dry.

"Because, easygoing people shouldn't do things they don't like to do."

"Oh, Mitch, do you have a book of these rules or do you come up with them on your own?" She stretched the long telephone cord into the laundry room.

"What was that noise?"

"What noise?"

"I hear water running."

"Oh, that. I started the washer." Raine never sat still when she was on the phone. For her, talking on the telephone wasn't an excuse to relax. "So, we've established that I do indeed like football."

"The Eagles are playing the Bears this weekend and I have season tickets. Wanna go?"

In his living room across town, Mitch stretched his legs out, propped one bare foot over the other and rotated his shoulders. Tanner lifted his head and Mitch obliged him, scratching behind the dog's long ears. He'd heard noises in the background throughout the conversation, and wondered what Raine was doing. She sure as hell wasn't relaxing. She wasn't hanging on his every word, either.

"If you have other plans or don't feel like going, we could do something else."

"I don't have other plans."

"And?"

"And, I'd love to go. Do you want me to see if Clarissa or Julie want to come along? It would be a great way for you to meet one of them."

He let out a slow breath, being careful not to let her hear. He did not want her to bring along one of her single friends. He wanted to be alone with her, dammit.

"Sure, why not. I'll pick you, and whoever else is interested, up around one on Sunday."

"One o'clock will be *fine*."

He didn't understand the reason for the slight groan that followed her statement, but it didn't matter. He replaced the phone, feeling enormously annoyed. Going on a date with Raine and her friend was not exactly how he wanted to spend his Sunday afternoon. Unfortunately, he couldn't think of any other way to continue seeing her.

On Sunday, Mitch's "around one" turned out to be closer to two. Trying the handle on Raine's front door, he was surprised to find it unlocked. He knocked, anyway, then walked into Raine's home. He finally found her on the second floor, so engrossed in her flight manual she didn't hear him. It was the first time he'd seen her completely still.

Mitch's ego hadn't taken such a beating in years. She obviously hadn't been walking the floors, waiting for him to arrive. Did she even care that he had?

Then she looked at him, round brown eyes meeting his, and he saw what he'd seen the first time he'd looked into her face. She was beautiful. Not stop-in-your-tracks glamorous, but subtle, heart-squeezing, blooming-before-your-eyes beautiful.

He lowered Joey to his feet, and before he could say a word, she jumped up, moving naturally, gracefully, on full power. "You couldn't find a sitter for Joey?"

"I found a sitter, but then I canceled. I decided it wouldn't be a bad idea to see how Joey felt about one of your single friends." Looking around, he asked, "Where is your single friend, anyway?"

She gave Joey a warm smile and a quick kiss, then hurried around the room, explaining that both her friends had plans for the afternoon. In a flurry of activity, she fluffed a sofa pillow and straightened the magazines on the coffee table before finally reaching for her jacket which was draped across a chair.

"Even easygoing people keep their doors locked in the city, Raine."

He saw surprise widen her eyes, and felt like a heel. Good grief, maybe his Aunt Millie was right. Maybe he was turning into an ornery, crotchety old bachelor already.

"I usually do. But I slipped out to feed the neighbor's cats, and I thought you'd be here any minute, so I didn't lock it again. How was I supposed to know you were going to be late?"

For a minute there, he hadn't thought she'd noticed his tardiness. But of course she'd noticed. Nothing got past her. Rather than being angry, she was patient. The last woman he'd been seeing had come unglued when he was late. Mitch wouldn't mind seeing Raine come unglued, in his arms, in his bed. He wondered how long she'd be patient there.

An antique clock chimed two o'clock from a corner across the room, and Joey ran to investigate. Mitch squatted next to his son, whose little fingers could disassemble intricate objects faster than any skilled craftsman anywhere. "You have a mantel clock sitting on the floor?"

"I don't have a mantel."

"Makes perfect sense to me."

She'd lowered to her knees near him, and he watched as her gaze traveled over his face, searching his eyes. "This clock belonged to my parents. They received it from my grandparents for their first anniversary. It's one of the few pieces I brought with me from the old house."

Without closing her eyes, Raine relived the anguish she'd felt those first years without her parents. "This clock has always reminded me of my mother and father, but my brush with death two months ago brought their deaths back in vivid detail. The little girl and I were rushed to the hospital, where everything I heard, everything I saw, reminded me of the last moments of my mother's life.''

Mitch and Joey both went perfectly still. Entranced by the depth and feeling in her voice, Mitch felt as if he were on the brink of understanding. His heart thudded, feeling heavy. "You were with your mother when she died?" he whispered.

She nodded. "I'll never forget the pain in her eyes, the sadness at having to leave us behind. She asked me to keep the family together. I wanted to take the sadness away, and there was only one way to do that."

Her voice had dropped in volume and her words squeezed his heart like a turning fist. Her eyes darkened, and Mitch wanted to pull her into his arms, for so many reasons. "So you promised your mother."

Raine nodded, and Mitch didn't say any more. That promise to her mother had cost Raine her freedom. No wonder she wanted to recapture it now. No wonder he was so drawn to this woman.

Raine wanted freedom and fun. Well, he was just the person to show her both.

If he'd known her single friend wouldn't be joining them, he wouldn't have canceled Joey's sitter. He would have done everything in his power to make this afternoon perfect. A sunny September afternoon, a football game, a cup of coffee in an out-of-the-way café. A stolen kiss that would lead to another, which would lead to his place, or hers. . . .

Showing her how carefree he was wasn't going to be easy. And it had little to do with the fact that Joey was along. It was because suddenly, Mitch didn't feel all that carefree. What he was feeling was pure desire, the kind that strummed, slow and heavy, all through his body, desire that one thing, and one thing only would satisfy.

She averted her eyes and stood, and for a moment, Mitch was afraid she'd read the longing in his eyes, but all she said was, "We're going to be late."

"We're already late."

"An hour late! Do you realize I've never been an hour late for anything in my life?"

"You have now." He lifted Joey on his way up, and Raine darted ahead of them, leading the way down the stairs. By the time they'd reached the bottom step out front, she was in the middle of telling him about the dilemma she faced each time she tried to feed the neighbor's cats. "Ansel attacks me and Percy won't come out from underneath the china cabinet. Are we driving this to the game?" She pointed to the sporty silver truck parked along the curb.

"How do you do that?" He took her hand to slow her steps.

"Do what?"

"How do you notice every minute detail in the blink of an eye?"

Raine breathed lightly between parted lips. Her gaze met his, but she didn't answer his question. Her palm fit perfectly in his, and her pulse fluttered in her wrist, tripping the regular rhythm of her breathing. She was naturally observant, but her awareness of Mitch went beyond that.

She tugged her hand from his and was relieved when he let it go easily. Relieved, and a bit amazed. He'd placed no demands on her, in spite of the fact that he'd suddenly found himself with a two-year-old, when he obviously had little experience caring for a child of any age, in spite of the fact that she'd offered to help.

Her phone had rung a dozen times this past week, most of the calls from people asking for advice, or at least needing her to lend them a listening ear. Tammy Hart, who ran Hart's Day Care, had asked Raine to baby-sit her baby while she took her three-year-old to the zoo. Mildred Crandel, who was going through a painful divorce, had called twice to cry. Raine had spoken to her old friend from high school, Clarissa Cohagan, who had called to chat. Clay and Holly had both needed a favor, and her neighbor had called to inquire after her cats.

Raine had gladly helped with each of their problems. She'd consoled, advised and listened. And she'd thought of Mitch a hundred times. His was a *take-it-or-leave-it* attitude, and theirs should have been the perfect friendship.

The problem was, Raine didn't feel simple friendship for him. She liked him, and she'd missed him, in a more-than-friendly way. She'd also missed Joey. How was she ever going to become a free spirit when she grew attached to people so easily?

He'd tucked Joey into the car seat between them, refusing her offer of help with a steady smile and strict orders to relax and enjoy herself. There was nothing in his words that should have triggered romantic thoughts, yet they came to her mind immediately. And the sight of his long fingers looped casually around the steering wheel made her wonder how they'd feel on her skin.

"Is this your truck?" she asked, trying for a *friendly,* conversational tone.

"Taylor needed my car tonight," he began. "So we switched. I could have made the trade with you along, but then I would have had to explain that we're only friends. Taylor wouldn't have believed me, and by tonight he and Kyle would both be calling."

His relationship with his brothers intrigued her. Leaning down to retrieve Joey's toy from the floor, she asked, "What do you mean? Why would they both be calling you tonight?"

"You don't want to know."

"Of course I do."

"All right. You asked for it. Kyle would want to know what you look like. And they'd both ask how you are in bed."

Her gaze flew to his. "No!"

One side of his mouth quirked, and Raine found something warm, almost enchanting, in his humor. Her body had responded to the briefest mention of sharing a bed with Mitch, warming her most hidden places. "You don't really tell one another, do you?"

"I've been known to kiss and tell. But I haven't mentioned you."

Raine was pretty sure she should have been glad, and didn't like the fact that she was a little disappointed. No matter how many times she told herself she didn't want a relationship, no matter how many times she'd promised herself she'd find adventure in other ways, it always came back to this. Every time Mitch's gaze met hers, her heart turned over. Every time he looked into her eyes, she felt on the verge of adventure.

"I think we're making progress, Raine." His voice was deep, as if he'd been partaking in a little fantasy of his own.

"Progress?"

"You haven't jiggled your foot throughout this entire conversation."

"That's because I'm learning to relax." Raine's gaze slid to her narrow black shoe then to the road ahead. "I've always wanted to see one of those!"

"Always wanted to see what?"

"An estate sale. I've never been to one and we just passed a sign that said, Turn Right Next Mile."

Half a minute later, Mitch slowed the truck down. "What are you doing?" she asked him.

"I'm turning right. You said you wanted to see an estate sale. Let's go."

"But what about the game? What about your season tickets?"

"Easygoing people go with the flow."

His words were teasing, but his stare held a challenge. Her curiosity was aroused, among other things. "Mitch, I have to admit, I like your style." His style wasn't all she liked, but she wasn't about to admit that out loud.

Ten minutes later, he parked the truck along the road behind a long row of other vehicles. With Joey perched on Mitch's shoulders, they hurried toward the auctioneer, the steady loquacity of the man's voice echoing across the grounds. The sale was already underway.

"Five-dolla-dolla-dolla-dolla-five-dolla-dolla-do-I-he'-six?-Six-dolla-dolla-dolla-dolla . . ."

"This is going to be incredible!" Raine declared. "Where do we begin?"

Mitch steered her to the cashier's stand where a middle-aged trustee asked, "Did you both want a number this afternoon?"

Mitch answered, "One for the lady. I'm just going along for the ride."

"You're not bidding?" Raine asked him.

"I'll help you. First you have to look around, see what's going to be auctioned off, find something you want."

Raine led the way, inspecting antiques, assessing the crowd, determining how much money several items were worth, aware the entire time of the auctioneer's steady prattle. And of Mitch. He radiated a natural charm that drew her like a magnet. She still wasn't quite sure how they'd gone from football to an estate sale, but Mitch acted as if he'd planned it all along.

A dark wooden rocker caught her attention. "I'd like to bid on this," she whispered.

"Why are you whispering?" His own low murmur made her laugh, made her feel like a conspirator.

"Because, if those other people know how much I like this, they'll bid against me."

Raine took Joey's hand and watched as Mitch glided his palm across the rocking chair's smooth seat. There was no discounting the pleasure she felt when he straightened, shrugging his approval. "Try not to look too interested," he murmured.

In spite of her intentions, Raine's was the first bid, her voice giving her excitement away. After her bid had been raised several times, the auctioneer finally shouted, "Sold, for thirty-five dollars to number eighty-seven."

She laughed with delight as she threw her arms around Mitch's neck. The split second it took to breathe in his pine scent, to feel the roughness of his cheek against her hair, her laughter faded. She raised her chin and her gaze locked with his. In that moment, the week and a half they'd been apart seemed like a very long time.

She doubted she'd ever forget the invitation in his eyes, or the promise in his smile. The auctioneer had started the bidding on another piece of furniture, one she'd intended to bid on. But, by the time she'd untangled her arms from around his neck and had put a little distance between them, by the time her heartbeat had returned to normal, the auctioneer shouted, "Sold! To number forty-three."

An hour and a half later, Mitch leaned against a wooden post. Joey was having the time of his life poking through a pail filled with sand, and Mitch was thoroughly enjoying watching Raine scurry from one area to the next, assessing everything from old pieces of furniture to useless knick-knacks to battered old engine parts. She reminded him of a small, beautiful bird, flitting from place to place, within his sight, but out of reach. It was the way she moved, like an exotic creature, her hair blowing against her cheek so utterly soft.

She scanned the crowd, her eyes roaming, searching, until they settled on him. He watched as a smile lifted her lips, a smile for him. Tightness started in his chest, then radiated lower. With every step she took toward him, his conviction increased. This bird wouldn't always flutter away from him. Someday, she'd fly to him. Someday soon.

Raine didn't stop talking about the sale all the way home. He'd never heard her laugh so much, and Mitch was sure he wasn't simply imagining that she was beginning to look more at ease. He understood that her desire for independence wasn't frivolous, but something she truly wanted and deserved. He'd also read the look of longing in her eyes, and felt a smug sense of satisfaction.

She turned in the seat and looked through the back window at her purchases, which were secured in the truck's bed. "How did I ever manage to buy all that stuff? Where will I put it?"

"Are you kidding? You're living room is practically empty. So is the dining room," he said, concentrating on backing Taylor's truck into the alley behind her house.

Just then, two young men came sauntering out of the house. Mitch instantly recognized one of them. "Thought you were going to the game," Clay said, before taking a large bite of a sandwich he held in his hand.

"We were sidetracked." Raine answered. Pointing to his sandwich, she laughed, "Did you leave any for me?"

"Jason needed something from home. There wasn't much to eat at his house and we're sick of cafeteria food, so we stopped here for a snack. Except for a freezer full of microwave dinners, this is all we could find."

Clay winked, and sauntered toward his friend's car. Irritation prickled along Mitch's spine as he watched the two young men drive away. Like the annoying thud of a Sunday hangover, Mitch's irritation grew. Clay, at least, didn't look totally unintelligent. It was pretty obvious Raine could have used his help carrying all this furniture inside. Instead of offering to help, he'd simply left, criticizing her lack of food at the same time. But what really rankled was that Raine didn't *ask* for her brother's help.

Joey, who'd missed his nap, had fallen asleep in his car seat, and Mitch and Raine were standing in the back of the truck, where he crossed his arms and leveled his gaze at her.

"I never would have let my brothers leave without helping."

She lowered herself to a trunk, her eyes falling away from his. "Your relationship with your brothers is different than my relationship with Clay."

Mitch remembered the look on her face when she'd watched Clay walk away. "Relationships are two-way streets, you know."

"I can't ask anything of Holly and Clay. They were both so young and sad and lost when our parents died, but Clay suffered the most. He was eleven years old, on the brink of adolescence. School had never come easy to him, but that year, he really faltered. He and I spent hours each night on homework. I was so worried about him, about both of them, I couldn't ask them for anything. I still can't."

"You were too young for that kind of responsibility, you know." He took both her hands in his, running his thumb over her smooth skin. He read *need* in her eyes. She was vulnerable, dammit. Open-eyed open-soul vulnerable.

"You don't have to help, either, Mitch."

A few things about Raine McAlister were beginning to make sense. She wore her heart on her sleeve, offered her help unquestioningly. But she didn't ask for anything in return. When it came to needing someone, she kept her distance. No strings.

She said she needed freedom. Mitch wondered if she realized she needed more than that. He'd give her that freedom she so coveted. He'd also give her fun, laughter and a helluva lot more—if she'd let him.

Releasing her hand, he stepped back. "I hope you're strong, because if you're not, I'm going to have a hard time carrying this junk up all those stairs by myself."

"Junk! Priceless antiques," Raine stated in an admonishing tone.

"And what do you call this?" Mitch rested his palm along the rim of an old metal pail.

"I only wanted the antique fern stand. Don't you think it was pretty underhanded of them to include that old pail filled with—" she'd almost said junk "—stuff in the bargain?"

"Very underhanded," he agreed, his slow grin giving way to a deep chuckle.

Striking a pose, she flexed the muscles in her arm. "Don't worry, I'm strong as an ox. A regular Amazon. We'd better hurry, Mitch, if we want to get all this...this...these priceless antiques inside before it rains."

Mitch looked up at the sky where thick, dark clouds were moving in.

The clouds dawdled overhead until nearly everything, including one sleeping two-year-old, had been carried inside, and up at least one flight of stairs. When the first sprinkles pattered against the windows, Raine smiled. Intense pleasure at the way her house was filling up, becoming a home, shone in her eyes.

While Mitch relaxed on an old trunk, waiting for her to decide where she wanted to put it, she sat down on the wooden rocker. The chair squeaked each time she rocked, the sound lulling her movements, slowing them, creak by steady creak.

Mitch's eyes lazily regarded her. His look was sensuous, toe-curling sensuous, and she let her gaze travel just as extensively, nearly as lazily, over him. His light brown hair curled over his forehead, saddle tan tresses touching the back neckline of his navy sweatshirt. His eyebrows were straight and even above deep blue eyes that dipped down the tiniest bit at the corners. His nose was masculinely broad, his lips wide, a dark stubble deepening the color of his chin.

Raine remembered the rasp of his jaw against her cheek, and wished she could kiss the curve of his lips. She wondered what he expected, what he wanted. She could live with the wanting, but the expectations scared her, enough to break the ribbon of desire that connected them.

She sprang to her feet, the chair creaking in protest. "As cute as you look on that trunk, I don't think it looks quite right in the middle of the floor."

He rose to his feet slowly. "I haven't been referred to as cute since my permanent teeth came in."

At that moment, Mitch didn't look cute. Teddy bears and puppies were cute. Soft things were cute, and Mitch didn't look soft. He looked lean and rugged. And hard. And he was gazing at her as if he had only one thing on his mind.

After a lingering silence, she whispered, "This is beginning to look like a living room." She spread her arms wide, her gesture sweeping the entire area.

For a laid-back kind of guy, Mitch moved fast. He was suddenly next to her, sliding his hand to her waist, his fingers somehow finding their way beneath her shirt. She grasped his arms, then spread her fingers over his shirt, measuring the width of his shoulders. He felt hard and solid and masculine.

For several moments, he simply held her eyes with his own. Then he lowered his mouth to her face, his lips brushing her forehead and cheek like the rasp of a husky whisper. Her eyelids fluttered down, and she was flooded with sensations, the softness of his mouth, the warmth of his breath, the sound of his breathing.

She spread her fingers wide, winding them into the soft curls at his neck, aware of his ragged breathing, aware of every inch of him, of every hard muscle. His lips covered her mouth, and he made a sound deep in his throat. The sound, dark and primitive, weakened her knees like a flame melting wax.

She met his kiss the way she did everything, full power, head-on. When his hands slid around to her back, pulling her tight against him, she fit herself to the contours of his hard body.

Raine felt as if she were perched on a narrow cliff, treacherously close to the edge, ready to jump into the unknown. His warm breath worked magic on her skin. There was more magic every place they touched. And it was pushing her closer, ever closer, to the edge.

The sound of raindrops tripping across the windowpanes brought her to her senses. She straightened, lightening the kiss before ending it completely. Pressing her forehead to his cheek, she inhaled. He smelled faintly of after-shave, fresh air and early-autumn breezes. He'd somehow managed to chase away her common sense. She remembered an old saying that went something like: Love enhances all senses but dulls the common.

This has absolutely nothing to do with love.

Clearing that thought from her mind, she said, "I'm pretty sure easygoing people shouldn't kiss that way."

"That rule isn't in my book."

"No doubt. But seriously, I don't think—"

"I don't think, either. Not when you kiss me like that."

"That's another thing, Mitch. Friends shouldn't kiss the way we just kissed."

He took her hand and glanced up the stairway, showing her without words where he wanted to go with her. "I'd say we passed friendship a while ago, wouldn't you?"

They both glanced at Joey, who was beginning to move on the sofa nearby. Keeping her eyes trained on the child, Raine said, "I thought you wanted me to introduce you to my single friends."

"So, introduce me," Mitch replied. "In the meantime, I'd like to continue seeing you. You don't want a serious relationship, anyway, so the fact that we won't be seeing each other, exclusively, shouldn't be a problem."

Joey sat up and popped his thumb in his mouth, and Raine realized that, by waking up, he'd saved her from making a decision regarding Mitch. The irony of the situation wasn't lost on her. She wanted to be free of responsibilities, and Mitch was facing a lifetime of them. The same adorable child who kept her from sharing an incredible adventure with Mitch had woken up before she'd had to explain why she couldn't fall in love with him. And since she hadn't *had* to explain, she and Mitch could have a little more time together before they went their separate ways.

Mitch plucked Joey from the sofa, and shot a look at the trunk sitting in the middle of the living-room carpet. "I'll take that upstairs for you anytime you want, Raine. Any time, any way."

Raine knew what he was saying, but for the life of her, she didn't know how to respond. He still hadn't placed any demands on her, and she just plain didn't know how to treat someone who didn't make demands.

Eyeing the trunk, and the narrow staircase, she reached one conclusion: before she took Mitch upstairs, *if* she took Mitch upstairs, she'd have to tell him this could only be a fling. She'd have to make it clear that she couldn't be tied down, not again, not now. Maybe not ever.

"I'm not going to take that trunk up to my bedroom."

"You're not?"

"No, I'm going to take it out to the garage, and I'm going to refinish it."

"Do you know anything about refinishing furniture?"

"No, but I'm going to try it. After all, we laid-back people should always be ready to try new things."

"Where did you hear that?"

"From the king of the laid-back."

He smoothed a lock of hair from her cheek and, looking deep into her eyes, murmured, "I figured you'd been paying attention."

She followed Mitch down the stairs, and at the back door, he turned and, with Joey on his hip, kissed her once more. Raising his mouth from hers, he said, "Have dinner with me Saturday."

She'd promised herself adventure and freedom, but that was before she'd discovered the passion beneath Mitch's kisses. She'd never sensed that kind of hunger before.

Maybe, if she didn't hurt anyone, she could experience more than one kind of adventure.

"All right," she answered, aware of what she was doing, aware that she was preparing to take a flying leap, and that she wasn't the only one who knew it.

"I'm going to talk to Julie and Clarissa again, see if I can set up a time for you to meet them."

Mitch smiled a self-confident smile. "Whatever you say. In the meantime, I'll see you Saturday around seven."

She called goodbye to Joey, and Mitch began to whistle. She waited to close the door until he'd ambled down the back steps, his shoes splashing through the puddles along the sidewalk. Pushing the door shut, she leaned back against the solid frame.

The tune he'd been whistling lingered in her memory long after he drove away. Closing her eyes, she felt the melody wash over her like an early-autumn shower. Raine slowly began to climb the stairs once again, unaware that she'd begun to hum, picking up the softly lyrical song where Mitch's whistle had left off.

Chapter Five

"**I** really hate these computers," Mildred Crandel grumbled from across the room.

Raine looked up from the stack of files on her desk. "Don't let them intimidate you, Mildred."

Pushing to her feet, she rounded her desk, ready to help her co-worker. Truth be told, Raine wasn't thrilled about the new computers, either.

She leaned over her friend, who was pushing a key as if she had a death wish. "This computer thinks it's so smart," Mildred sputtered.

Just then, the machine started beeping, and Raine and Mildred both jumped back. Mildred practically screamed, and Raine's hands flew to her throat. With a sigh, Mildred said, "I just know it did that on purpose!"

Raine pushed a series of buttons, and the horrendous beeping stopped. "Don't be silly. Computers can't do anything on purpose. They're only as smart as the person who programmed them." Turning, she sauntered back to her own desk, and her own stack of work.

"Why, Raine McAlister! You've been humming that same tune for two days, and I've never heard you hum in all the years you've worked here. Don't tell me, after all this time, you're beginning to like your job!"

Raine looked over her shoulder, into Mildred Crandel's friendly face. Blowing a strand of hair from her eyes, she glanced at the files in front of her and said, "Mildred, I never said I didn't like it here."

"You didn't have to, dear. Some things don't need saying."

This was the first time since Mildred's husband had asked her for a divorce several months ago that the older woman had shown an interest in anything other than her own agony, and Raine thought it was a good sign. She just wished they could talk about something other than her job. Besides, she didn't hate her job, exactly. It just drove her slightly crazy. She'd have preferred to do something less sedate, something more varied, more exciting. She'd been reading the help-wanted ads since the middle of summer. But she hadn't told anyone from the office.

"If it isn't interest in your job that's making you hum, it must be a man."

On second thought, talking about her *job* didn't sound all that bad, a lot better, in fact, than discussing a certain man who made her feel like humming. "I'm just feeling good these days," Raine declared. "I love my new place, and the flying lessons are going great."

"So you haven't met someone new? Someone exciting and handsome and charming?" Mildred asked.

Unbidden, Mitch's image flashed through Raine's mind, his blue eyes and his slow, steady smile, his tall rugged body with its lean, muscled build. "I happen to know someone who fits your description, Mildred," Raine replied. "But he's looking for a wife, so I'm introducing him to my single friends."

"Good heavens, you really were serious when you said you wanted to be free, weren't you? My divorce will be final soon," Mildred declared, "and I'll be single. Tell me, Raine, how old is this man?"

"Thirty-five."

"Oh. I've been thinking about dying my hair back to blond, but I'm afraid thirty-five is still a little too young for me. If only I were twenty years younger."

Raine couldn't help but laugh at Mildred's wistful tone. "I already set him up with Larielle, from accounts receivable, but they didn't hit it off. I talked to another friend of mine about him yesterday, but she insisted she isn't interested in dating anyone, no matter how handsome, how exciting or how charming. So, I called Julie in personnel, and she was all for meeting him. When I told her he has a two-year-old son, she seemed skeptical, but she still agreed to go out with him."

"He has a little boy?" Mildred asked. "Oh, that could definitely complicate things."

Yes, Raine thought to herself. Having Joey definitely complicated matters where Mitch Harris was concerned.

After her conversation with Mildred on Friday, Raine had been careful not to hum out loud, but there was nothing she could do about the tune that kept running through her mind. It was still there Saturday evening as she stood in front of her closet.

She wished she'd asked Mitch where they were going for dinner. At least then she'd know how to dress. All her clothes were so mundane, so practical. She'd always purchased clothing that would last, never selecting trendy fashions or here-this-season-gone-the-next fads. Raine had a sudden desire to grab everything from her closet and march right down to the Salvation Army. Someone else would probably appreciate the clothes. After all, every single article looked nice, and she wanted to rid her wardrobe of clothing that looked either *nice* or *fine*.

Taking her panty hose in hand, she turned to the antique mirror she'd purchased at the estate sale. Why hadn't it ever occurred to her how boring her wardrobe was? Even her underclothes were plain, utilitarian. She smoothed the nylons up her legs, then turned back to her closet where she ran her hand over a tan skirt, its color basic, but the fabric soft and airy. It would have to do.

For all its neutrality, she didn't like the skirt with any blouse or sweater she put with it. Too plain, or too staid, or too drab. She remembered a black blouse she'd purchased at the beginning of summer, and pulled it from the back of the closet. The top was sleeveless, the shoulders slashed high. She hadn't worn it since the day before her near miss, hadn't worn anything that didn't cover up the thick scar on her upper arm.

With so few choices, she pulled the soft fabric over her head, marveling at the way it shimmered into place. She decided the scar wasn't all that noticeable, but the white straps of her bra were.

Now what? Raine tugged the top over her head, unfastened her bra and folded it neatly inside her top drawer. She slid her arms and head through the openings in the material then let the fabric glide over her skin. The blouse felt wonderful, almost like a caress everyplace it touched. Closing her eyes, she imagined Mitch's hands following the same path over her body.

Thoughts like this one had had her heart hammering in her chest all week. The memory of the invitation in his eyes was a heady sensation. The thought of making love with him sent anticipation racing through her, but the fact that he was looking for a permanent relationship, and she wasn't looking for any relationship, sent that anticipation jangling along her nerve endings. Those warring emotions made her feel the tiniest bit wild.

Raine couldn't remember feeling this way before a date, and decided it was because there was something different about Mitch. A few of the men she'd dated these past several years had been on the wild side, but with them, she'd known where it would end. She didn't know what to expect with Mitch; the not knowing was exciting. She wanted this brief interlude in her life, one that had no real beginning and no particular destination. But first, she had to make sure he understood.

The mantel clock chimed seven deep-toned notes from downstairs, and for once in her life, she didn't hurry. Mitch had said he'd be here at seven, but then, Mitch was always late. She took her time applying her makeup, took extra care styling her hair. By the time she'd fastened black earrings through her lobes and slipped her feet into black heels, it was 7:21. She smiled to herself when her doorbell rang a few minutes later. Mitch had perfect timing.

Standing in the open doorway, Raine smiled hello. He didn't return the greeting until his gaze had traveled over every inch of her. He was naturally unobservant, but she knew the exact moment he noticed she wasn't wearing a bra. It hadn't taken more than three seconds. His gaze flowed over her with open admiration, and although he may have tried not to stare, his eyes were repeatedly drawn below her shoulders.

"You look beautiful, Raine."

She'd never thought of herself as beautiful, but beneath his gaze, there was no denying that's exacly how she felt. He stepped forward and the desire in his eyes beckoned to her, turned her heart upside down and sent excitement dancing through her veins.

He kicked the door shut with just the right amount of force, and they slowly moved closer, until they were no more than a breath apart. His right hand found her waist, his left hand glided to her nape, tipping her head up. His lips met hers, drawing feelings from the bottom of her heart.

His kiss was hungry and persuasive, and it left her feeling boneless. He moved his lips to the hollow at the edge of her jaw, and Raine tilted her head to one side, resting her forehead in the curve of his shoulder.

It took every ounce of willpower Mitch possessed to keep from kissing her again. She was warm and pliant in his arms, ardent and passionate. She wanted what he wanted, but he wanted it to be perfect. Tonight it would be.

He breathed in deep, steadying breaths and relaxed his hold on her. "Ah, Raine, that was definitely worth the wait."

He wasn't quite smiling, and Raine's gaze was drawn to his lower lip. Without thinking, she ran her thumb over it, and beneath her touch, Mitch went perfectly still.

"That shade of lipstick does nothing for your tie," she whispered.

Mitch took a white handkerchief from his pocket and wiped it across his mouth. "How do I look?"

She eyed his gray jacket, his silver shirt and red tie, doubting the man had a self-conscious bone in his body. "You know exactly how you look. That's the trouble."

He didn't smile, but a sensuous light gleamed in his eyes. Her lips still tingled from his last kiss, yet she wanted to kiss him again. Instead, she voiced the thought that had been grating on her mind all week. "Mitch, I've been thinking. If you're really serious about finding the right woman, I don't think you should be wasting your time with me."

He stared directly into her eyes, and without blinking, said, "This is only one date, but believe me, I don't consider any time I spend with you wasted."

"Then you don't think I'll interfere with your looking for a wife?"

"Not in the least."

His gaze was serious, so was his tone of voice, so serious, in fact, that Raine knew he was telling the truth. He understood about her dreams. All he wanted was to spend a little time with her. Nothing burdensome, just some lighthearted fun.

"There is one thing I'd like you to do."

Raine felt hypnotized by the raw sensuality in his expression. "Yes?"

"Would you show me your view? The one where you can see for miles?"

His request awakened a response from deep within her. How could he have known there was nothing she'd like more than to show him her special place?

Forty minutes later, she instructed Mitch to park his car at the edge of a seldom-used path that wound through the Pocono Mountains. The evening breeze blew cool as they walked a short distance to a sturdy wooden fence near the top of the mountain.

"I haven't been up here in a long, long time. The people in my office call this the Near Country, but I call it heaven."

They stood side by side, elbows touching, their forearms resting along the wooden railing. The sun hung low in the sky, tinting the clouds a pale amber. All around them were trees, their leaves beginning to change from green to gold and red.

"Imagine what this will look like in a week or two, when the color reaches its peak." His voice was low, echoing with longings that had nothing to do with his words.

Raine lifted her chin from her hands and turned her head until she was gazing at his profile. After that kiss in her front hall, her heart had seemed to lodge in her throat. She felt tipsy, as if she were teetering on the edge of something magnificent.

"You aren't looking at the view," he whispered.

"I'm looking at one view."

The color of his eyes warmed to a deep blue. His voice dropped to an even deeper tone. "Raine, you look like someone stepping off an airplane without a parachute."

"I feel as if I'm taking a jump in the dark."

"I'd catch you."

Her gaze swept across the sky, over the hills covered with colorful trees, down to the meadow dotted with rocks and patches of weeds far below. A feeling of wonder floated over her, a kind of bottomless peace, the same feeling she experienced each time she gazed at this view. This time the feeling was intensified because she shared it with Mitch.

The air around them was charged with primitive awareness. Raine felt on the threshold of adventure, and didn't fully understand what held her back. "I believe you'd try to catch me, but I have to land on my own two feet. I have to take care of myself, first."

Mitch felt a pounding certainty that his next words would be crucial. He thought they'd gotten this out of the way in her front hall, when she'd asked if their relationship would interfere with his finding a wife. He'd known she'd watched him closely, and he'd spoken the truth; the time he spent with Raine in no way impeded his quest for a wife, because the more time he spent with her, the more certain he became that he didn't want to see anyone else.

Raine wasn't ready to hear that. So, choosing his words carefully, he raised his shoulders, and lifted his hands toward the sky. "I'm not about to tie you down, Raine. This can be anything you want it to be."

"Anything?"

He nodded, and she tipped her head to one side, as if contemplating the possibilities. "You mean this can be something fleeting, like a wonderful adventure?"

Mitch nodded again. He liked the sound of sharing an adventure with Raine. He didn't particularly care for the fleeting part, but if that's what she wanted, who was he to say no? And there was always the chance that he could change her mind.

She turned away and began to walk. He stayed where he was on the path, his hip resting against the railing. His gaze followed Raine as she strolled away from him, followed the course of the breeze as it blew through her airy skirt, pressing the fabric against her legs and back. Desire, rousing and heavy, clenched deep inside him.

Raine had strange ideas about freedom. She'd never expected anything from anyone. She gave and gave and gave. Even her smiles were given freely. Clay and Holly walked all over her, taking, taking, always taking. And Raine expected nothing in return. She fed the neighbor's cats, worked late at a job she didn't even like, listened to people's troubles and baby-sat for their children.

Mitch wanted to grasp her shoulders, to frame her face with his hands, to carry her up to the clouds. He wanted to give something to her. Freely, physically, emotionally. And she wanted to land on her own two feet.

At the curve in the path, Raine turned and the wind lifted the hair from her forehead. From the depths of her eyes Mitch saw a twinkle as elusive as a firefly. Still, she didn't hurry. She was changing. Before his eyes she was becoming carefree. In that instant, his feelings became crystal-clear. In that instant, he fell in love.

Now that he had a name for what he felt for her, he wanted her to love him back.

Watching her come nearer, Mitch slid his hand deep into his pocket where his fingers came into contact with his keys. With staccato-like movements, he jingled them against his loose change, the sound lost in the breeze.

She walked straight to him, reached up and brushed her lips across his, an erotic smile settling on her mouth. Mitch's body tightened in response. He took her hand, and together they wound their way back toward his car. By the time he'd opened the door, she wasn't the only one smiling.

Raine had felt as though she were floating all evening. After leaving the lookout, they had found a lovely restaurant. Dinner had been wonderful, the food cooked to perfection, the wine exquisite. Mitch's gaze had shimmered over her like satin sheets, meeting hers again and again, until she was sure she was infused with liquid heat. The brush of his fingers had been sensuous and deliberate, the caress of her touch along his arm equally so.

When he parked in the alley behind her house, he wasted no time pulling her from the car and kissing her before they'd made it up two steps. He kissed her again inside the back door, and once more in the laundry room where she dropped her purse.

His hands trailed down the satiny material of her blouse, and she shivered in response to his touch. She slipped her hands inside his jacket, her fingers gliding over his tie, spreading outward over his chest. She stepped out of her shoes, and for the first time in as long as she could remember, left them lying in the middle of the hall. Being carefree was wonderful. It was heady. It was more than she'd ever dreamed it would be.

The stairs were dark, and Raine took Mitch's hand in hers and led him up, up, ever closer to her bedroom. He stopped her once, pulled her close, then pressed her against the wall. He fit his lean body against hers, and kissed her again. Raine wrapped her arms around his neck and gave in to the passion swirling around them, between them, inside them.

He pressed his forehead to hers and stole another kiss. She couldn't see his face in the dark, but felt his smile on her own lips, felt it deep in her heart.

At the top of the first flight of stairs, Mitch turned her around and took her in his arms. "I can hardly wait. I want you, Raine." His voice was only a whisper, yet it rumbled deep in his chest. They took another step, and another kiss.

"Rainie, is that you?" A muffled voice called from the darkened living room.

Raine turned around, her eyes searching the darkness. "Holly?" She heard a sniffle, and a shuddering sob. "Holly, what is it?"

Her sister's voice came from someplace closer, raw with tears, aching with sadness. "Rainie, I'm pregnant."

"Okay, Holly," Raine said as she poured the liquid from the paper cup into the narrow tube. "Now we wait."

Holly waved the sheet of directions. "It says we have to wait ten minutes. I don't know if I can stand to wait another second!"

They left the kit in the bathroom and went up to the bedroom where Raine smoothed the wrinkles from the sheets on her bed while Holly traced heart patterns into the dust on the dresser top. "Everything's changing," Holly whispered. "Even you."

"What do you mean?" Raine asked, fluffing a pillow.

"I've never seen dust on your dresser before, or your slip on the floor. And I tripped over your shoes in the back hall."

Raine sat on the edge of her freshly made bed. Holly was right. She *was* changing. She was having the time of her life—taking flying lessons, refinishing her furniture, spending time with Mitch. But the results of Holly's test could bring it all tumbling down.

Running her hand across the yellow quilt, Raine didn't know what to say to her sister. How could she lecture Holly on casual sex when she and Mitch had been about to have just that? But, she reminded herself, nothing about their evening had been casual. Sensuous and intoxicating, intensely erotic and liberating, but definitely not casual. If Holly hadn't arrived, heaven only knew where pleasure would have taken them.

"I'm sorry I ruined your evening," Holly whispered.

Raine looked across the room at her sister. Their hair was nearly the same color of pale blond, but Holly's hung long and straight. Their faces were both heart-shaped. They both had large eyes, although Raine's were a deep brown, and

Holly's were dark blue, and glistening with unshed tears at the moment.

"Holly, you didn't ruin my evening."

"Hmmph. You weren't planning to spend the night tossing and turning with me."

Raine looked straight into Holly's eyes. "No. But you're my sister, and I'm glad you came to me."

Holly sniffled, and practically flew into her older sister's arms. "I don't know what I'd do without you," she cried.

Raine stroked Holly's hair and mumbled words of comfort. Last night she'd been hovering at the edge of an imaginary cliff, ready to take a jump into passion with Mitch. Today that cliff seemed miles and miles away.

"He was awfully cute."

Raine smiled in spite of the graveness of this situation. She knew Mitch didn't appreciate being referred to as cute.

"Will he be back? I mean, he left in an awful hurry. Do you think he's mad?"

"He'll be *fine*. He doesn't let too much get to him."

"Rainie? Is it time?"

Raine looked at her watch and shook her head. "A few more minutes." In any other situation, she would have smiled. Holly never had been as patient as she or Clay.

"What do you think I should do?" Holly asked.

"I think we should wait until we find out the results of your test before we talk about that, don't you?

A few minutes later, staring at the blue ring on the bottom of the test device, Holly whispered the same question. "What am I going to do?"

Raine closed her eyes as all her hopes of being carefree flew out the open bathroom window. The test was positive. Holly was pregnant.

At the sound of a car in her driveway, Raine stopped sanding the old trunk and peeked out the garage window to investigate. "I'm in here, Mitch," she called from inside the small garage. She swiped her palms on her jeans and looked up when he entered. "I didn't expect to see you tonight." She gave Tanner a pat and Joey a kiss on the cheek but steered clear of touching Mitch.

"Is she?"

Mitch was obviously not in the mood to beat around the bush. Raine knew what he meant. He was asking about Holly's pregnancy test. Of course he'd want to know. She'd thought about calling him after Holly went back to school yesterday, but for some reason, couldn't. She'd come so close to making love with him, came within a breath of being completely independent. Holly's situation changed everything.

"She is."

The expression on her face kept Mitch from sputtering the string of four-letter words winging through his brain. For two days he'd waited for her to call. She hadn't. Looking at her now, he doubted she'd planned to. Damn.

He'd suspected, almost from the beginning, that Raine was the woman he wanted to spend the rest of his life with. Sure, he'd met her at a difficult time in his life, a time when he'd just found out he had a son. But he'd never doubted his feelings, never doubted things would work out between them. He'd known she didn't want to make a commitment, but he'd been confident it was only a matter of time before she realized what she really wanted was him.

"You could have called." He wanted to take back the words the second they were out. He knew he sounded like a pouting husband, knew he had no right to be angry because she hadn't phoned him.

Everyone heaped their problems on Raine, and it ticked him off. But he'd be damned if he'd do the same, just as he'd be damned if he'd let her go now, when she was almost his.

Joey wiggled to get down, and after setting him on his feet, Mitch said, "We just dropped by to say hello. We've been walking in the park."

"From the looks of the three of you, I bet you did more running than walking."

A slow smile stretched his lips. "Tanner does like to run." The friendly dog plopped down on the cool concrete as if he'd had all the exercise he could stand for one day. To Mitch's amazement, Joey did the same.

Bending his knees, Mitch dropped to his haunches, the worn fabric of his jeans stretching across his muscled thighs. He ran his hand over the surface of the trunk. "You're doing a great job on this old wood."

Raine kneeled opposite him, watching him caress the smooth surface. He had broad hands, with knobby knuckles and long fingers. She ran her fingertip along the edge of one particularly nasty-looking scrape. "How could a dentist's hands be so rough? What do those patients do to you?"

"Except for an occasional bite, they're pretty harmless. They aren't to blame for my beat-up hands. These scrapes and callouses come from my weekly basketball games with Kyle and Taylor."

"Is that why you're so relaxed? Because you get the proper exercise?"

His hand stilled beneath hers. "All the proper exercise in the world wouldn't have helped me relax Saturday night."

As casually as she could manage, she murmured, "Me, neither." She'd tossed and turned all night long after Mitch had left. Holly had thought it was because she'd been worried about her. That was only part of the reason. Disappointment was the real reason she couldn't sleep. Disappointment, and the feeling that everything she wanted was out of her reach.

"If exercise is the key to relaxation, I should be lethargic tonight after walking halfway home from the airport."

"Where's your car?"

"It broke down," she explained.

"So you walked?"

She nodded, and Mitch jumped to his feet and paced across the few feet of uncluttered floor. "Alone? For heaven's sake, Raine, don't you read the newspapers?"

She grasped the sandpaper and took up where she'd left off before he'd arrived, smoothing away the remaining splinters. "I'm *fine,* Mitch."

"You're lucky." He stomped over to where she was working and placed his big, battered hand over her smooth one. "Why didn't you call someone?"

"I wasn't afraid. It wasn't that far and I didn't know who to call." Holly's latest worry had taken the wind from Raine's sails. How could she explain that she didn't know who to turn to?

"Why didn't you call me?"

"You wouldn't have been home if I had called. You just said you were in the park with Joey and Tanner."

"But you didn't even try."

"I'm not used to relying on anyone but myself, Mitch."

"Easygoing people call a friend when in need. The most important rule of all."

Her gaze was drawn to his hand resting over hers. Even though her skin tingled beneath his, he didn't press for more contact. Physically, they were on the brink of becoming more than just friends, but emotionally, he wasn't pushing her. He didn't ask for anything. It was because he didn't ask, didn't demand, that her eyes, when raised to his, filled with trust.

Mitch picked up a piece of sandpaper and began to help her remove the trunk's old finish. They talked about her job, which she disliked more with every passing day, about her flying lessons and about his patients. He didn't ask what Holly planned to do now that her suspicions were confirmed. Nor did he tell Raine about the phone calls he'd been receiving from Eva Russell, Joey's grandmother.

"Mitch," she murmured. "You would have loved the view from the plane tonight. The world seemed to slide away in every direction. It was incredible." She jumped to her feet and spun around. Tanner raised his head at the commotion then lowered it again as if he realized it was only Raine, on the wing again.

For the next half hour, they worked on the trunk, the silence stretching between them. She'd need him for a ride to work in the morning, but she didn't ask him. He'd given her every opportunity, nonchalantly steered the conversation in that direction several times. But she hadn't asked. He wanted her to need him, but she thought relying on someone would clip her wings. He didn't know how to show her that needing someone wouldn't necessarily tie her down, not if that someone was him.

"Come on, Joey, Tanner. Let's go home." Tanner stretched long and hard before coming to his feet.

"Mitch?"

Ask, dammit.

"They say you can tell a lot about a person by watching his dog."

Mitch hoped his disappointment didn't show. "Tanner, old buddy, I don't know which of us has just been more insulted."

Her laugh was marvelous, low and vibrant and sultry. It spread over him like syrup. She reached her hand toward him, her palm grazing his forearm. The eyes that stared into his were wide and sincere. "That wasn't an insult, Mitch. That was an extremely sincere compliment."

He didn't smile, couldn't have if his life had depended on it. He didn't know how to react. Hell, he'd never been in love before. Not like this. Not so that another person's needs came before his own.

He leaned toward her and grazed her mouth with his lips. Both their eyes remained open, giving the kiss a fleeting quality. Lifting his face from hers, he murmured, "Good night, Raine."

Joey and Tanner ran ahead, but Mitch walked the short distance to his car, aware that she was flipping off the light and closing the garage door. With quick movements, she ran up the steps and turned to wave once more.

That woman had him turned upside down and inside out. What he really wanted to do was follow her inside, up those two flights of stairs, to her bedroom. Just thinking about what he wanted to do, how he wanted to touch her, sent tightness to places in his body he'd be better off not thinking about.

Mitch settled Joey in his car seat and bending over, coaxed Tanner into the back seat. A long wet tongue darted up the entire right side of Mitch's face. It wasn't the kind of kiss Mitch had in mind. Wiping his cheek with his shirt, he said, "Tanner, a bird in the hand is supposed to be worth two in the bush."

Not this time. Before this bird could be his, she had to be free.

Chapter Six

Raine glanced at her watch and blew her hair from her eyes in exasperation. She didn't have time to dawdle. As it was, she wasn't sure she'd make it to work on time. A horn blared behind her. Instead of turning to look, she increased her pace.

A series of catcalls rent the air, and although she didn't stop walking, Raine found herself glancing back in spite of her resolve not to. It was the high, incredibly raucous wolf whistle that stopped her in her tracks. That and the fact that it came from Mitch, who was parked at the curb not more than six feet away.

For once in her life, she didn't know what to say. She stood there for a moment, staring at him. His window was down, and she finally asked, "Mitch Harris, what in the world are you doing?"

"I'm enjoying the view, if you know what I mean. Don't just stand there, Raine. Get in, or we'll both be late for work. You know how I hate being late."

Raine hurried around to the other side of the car and climbed inside. "Since when do you hate being late?"

Mitch answered by putting the pedal to the floor. When both their heads rolled against the high-backed seats, Raine began to laugh. "Those catcalls really had me going."

"What do you mean?" he asked, pulling into the parking lot behind her office in record time.

"I've had a terrible morning. If I didn't know better, I'd say a tornado ripped through my house during the night. I've been so busy lately, I haven't had time to clean. And the laundry is spilling from the hamper."

"Doesn't sound so unusual to me."

"It doesn't even bother you, does it? Everything bothers me. My job is driving me crazy. So is my hair. My birthday is this weekend. I'm going to be so old. And for some reason, I suddenly don't like any of my clothes. I had absolutely nothing to wear to work this morning. And then to top it all off, I had to walk..."

"You'd look great in absolutely nothing."

His look was so pulse-pounding sensuous she forgot what she was saying. By the time his gaze had finished its journey over her body and returned to her face, her lashes had swept down.

"I can't stop thinking about you," he murmured. "I want you. If we didn't both have to be at work in a few minutes, I'd show you just how beautiful I find you."

Raine felt on the verge of tears, and never in her life had she cried at the drop of a hat. Holly's pregnancy had come out of the blue, adding to Raine's worries in a way she'd never expected.

She raised her watery eyes to find Mitch gazing at her. He cocked his head to one side, a smile pulling his lips upward. A sexy smile, but a smile just the same.

As always, that smile of his made her feel better, better than she'd felt since Holly had called out in the darkness Saturday night. With feelings pulling at her heart, she smiled back at him. "Everyone at work thinks I'm fidgety enough already. Now I don't know how I'm going to get through the rest of my day."

"Don't waste your time taking a cold shower. I've tried it a couple of times since Saturday night. It hasn't helped."

He covered her hand with his. Glancing at his lap, she knew what his restraint was costing him, and knew of one activity that would help. Unfortunately, neither had time for that kind of help. Trying to lighten the mood, she teased, "I don't think you should be wielding a high-speed drill today, Mitch, not in the condition you're in."

He almost smiled, and she half expected him to say something provocative. Instead, he said, "It's not too late, Raine. It's not too late to let life happen to you, to let yourself go."

The tears were back in her eyes, but she didn't let them fall. "I think you're wrong about that, Mitch. I think it is too late."

Mitch watched her close the door, watched her walk into her office building, trying to steady his erratic thoughts. There had to be a way to show her she could still be carefree.

By lunchtime, he'd come up with an idea. Wandering from the racks of dresses to the displays of sweaters, he thought his idea was a pretty good one at that. The saleswoman was helping a gray-haired woman near the front of the boutique, so he browsed at his leisure.

What had Raine said that morning? Everything was driving her crazy. Her job, her hair, her wardrobe, her birthday.

He thought her hair looked fabulous. Full on top, wispy on the bottom, practically inviting him to run his fingers through it. He couldn't help her with her job, but for her birthday he'd buy her something beautiful to wear. He had in mind a dress that was short and tight and black, or maybe the deepest shade of purple he could find.

Just thinking about Raine in those colors sent his imagination running wild. It must have been his imagination that had him gliding his hands over satin and lace in the palest colors he'd ever seen. He hadn't intended to look in this department, didn't even know how he'd ended up in the lingerie section in the first place.

With his heart hammering in his ears, Mitch placed a weightless satin teddy over his arm, and imagined smoothing his hand over the soft material, the fabric caressing Raine's supple body. Before he let his thoughts get too far, he made his way toward the front of the boutique. Looking around him, he wondered where all the shoppers had come from. The store was suddenly crawling with women.

He tried to look nonchalant as he stood in line at the counter, but he was aware of the women's curious stares. After all, he was the only man in the boutique, and the peach-colored teddy nestled in the crook of his arm was a definite contrast to his dark jacket.

Mitch considered throwing some money at the cashier and getting out of there. As fast and painlessly as possible. Then he realized he'd paid for Joey's day care with the rest of his cash. He'd have to stand in line like everyone else.

"What a lovely teddy!" the salesclerk said in the loudest, shrillest voice Mitch had ever heard.

He silently handed her his charge card and stared straight ahead until she returned it to him.

"Peach blush is such a lovely color, don't you think?" the woman chattered.

Mitch muttered something under his breath. The woman behind him smiled, the two behind her giggled. No wonder he'd never given a woman lingerie. Then he imagined Raine in the teddy. For her, he'd even go through this ordeal again.

* * *

Raine was on the garage floor, sanding the surface of her antique trunk, but her mind wasn't really on her task. Joey, who was playing with the pail of sand she'd received as part of the bargain along with her antique fern stand, wasn't the reason she couldn't concentrate. When Mitch had shown up unexpectedly earlier and offered to take a look at her car's engine, she'd told him she'd be happy to watch Joey while he worked.

"Even-steven?" he'd asked.

She'd simply nodded, but Joey had chirruped, "Even-steven," clapping his hands at his cleverness.

No, Joey had nothing to do with the reason she couldn't concentrate. Nor was it the loud clangs and clanks coming from her driveway. Mitch's cheerful, slightly off-key whistle was the reason her heart was thumping in her chest.

She cast a quick look at Joey, then at the boy's father. All she could see of Mitch, who was bent over her car's engine, was his backside. There was something about him tonight. He'd sauntered into the garage where she was working, given her one of his once-over smiles and sauntered out again. That had been nearly an hour ago.

He looked just as comfortable bending over her car as he did every other time she'd seen him. But there was more to him tonight than his usual nonchalant style. There was more spring in his step, more trill in his whistle.

Raine couldn't stand another minute. "Come on, Joey. This has gone on long enough." She dropped the sandpaper and leapt to her feet. Plucking Joey up, she settled him to her hip and hurried outside. Mitch turned his head in her direction. The whistle faded from his lips, replaced by a slow, secret smile.

"Well?" she asked.

He returned his attention to the engine, fiddled with this, fidgeted with that. "Turn the key," he instructed.

She placed Joey on her lap in the front seat and turned the key in the ignition. Nothing happened.

Mitch closed the hood. Sauntering around to the side, he said, "I have no idea what's wrong with your car. Never have been very good with them. That's always been Taylor's department."

"Then what have you been doing for the past hour?"

He smiled at her, but didn't answer her question.

"Mitch, you look like the cat who swallowed the canary. Are you going to tell me what's going on?"

He peered at her through the open window, reached for Joey, but didn't utter a word. It took Raine a few moments to notice the package nestled on the seat a few feet from her.

"What's this?"

"Come inside and find out." Mitch was already carrying Joey toward the back steps. Raine grasped the lightweight package and decided she had little choice but to follow.

Inside, Mitch ducked into the bathroom to scrub his and Joey's hands, taking an unbelievably long time even for a casual kind of guy. When he finally joined her, she asked, "Mitch, what is this?"

"It's an early birthday present. After you've opened it, you'll understand why I'm giving it to you early."

Joey started up the steps, and Raine followed, feeling like a kid at Christmas. At the top, she gazed into Mitch's eyes, his excitement mirroring her own. "Did you wrap this yourself?"

"Candace helped. I didn't tell her what's inside. She sputtered and said I'm beginning to remind her of Kyle. Coming from her, that was no compliment!"

Raine laughed at his saucy grin then plucked the purple bow from the box. "Tell me, Mitch, is Candace single?"

For once, Mitch seemed to be following her thought processes. "She's single, but don't even think it. I've known her for five years, and there's never been so much as a spark."

"Too bad," she murmured, being careful not to rip the colorful balloon paper. She raised the lid and pulled an envelope from several layers of tissue paper. She opened the envelope and her features became animated.

Holding two tickets for a hot air balloon ride in the palm of her hand, she exclaimed, "I've always wanted to ride in a balloon." She brushed her lips over his with a butterfly touch. "Thank you, Mitch."

He captured her fingers in his hand. "There's more."

Raine swallowed the flicker of apprehension that ran through her and burrowed through the layers of tissue paper until her fingers came into contact with satin and lace. Joey grabbed the box, and Mitch just managed to pull the teddy from inside before the child toddled away, box and all.

"The salesclerk called this color peach blush." Mitch saw the smile slip from her face to be replaced a moment later with an artificial one. Something was wrong. "Raine, what's the matter?" he said, worried.

"Nothing. It's beautiful."

A slap would have been less painful than such an untruth. Mitch's gaze narrowed on her face. "I've been imagining you in this all afternoon. Raine . . ."

She jerked to her feet and sprang away from him. Halfway across the room, she turned to confront him. "Look, Mitch, I appreciate the gifts. Really I do."

One of his least favorite four-letter words slipped from his mouth. Mitch grimaced when Joey repeated it from the other side of the room. He studied her for a long moment from the sofa, then slowly stood. The sense of disappointment he felt at her reaction was acute. Striding to the middle of the floor, he said, "You know I want you. I can't believe I only imagined you want me back. I wasn't imagining what almost happened between us Saturday night."

She spun away from him again. When she perched on the arm of the wooden rocker, her foot instantly began to jiggle. Mitch ran his fingers through his hair then slid his hand into his pocket. His fingers came into contact with his loose change, and he began rattling it in perfect time with Raine's foot.

"You're right," she began. "You didn't imagine what almost happened between us Saturday night. But that was between two carefree adults."

"So is this." He lifted the hand that held the teddy.

Raine didn't know how to explain what she was feeling. "These tickets are a wonderful gift."

"And this?" He held up the scrap of satin.

"It's beautiful, Mitch."

"But," he prodded. "Come on, Raine. Tell me what's wrong."

She took so long to answer, Mitch wondered if she would. "I don't want to hurt your feelings."

"I can take it. What I can't take is a lie between us. You like the tickets, and this teddy is beautiful, but what?"

"But it's like a rope anchoring that balloon to the ground. It makes me feel obligated."

"Obligated?" he asked absently.

"To ask you along." She held up the tickets and pointed at the teddy in his hand. "Obligated to wear the, the... Obligated to go to bed with you."

Terrible regrets assailed him. He never should have put the two gifts together. Now he was afraid he'd pushed her too far. Too fast. He didn't know what to say, how to make everything right. "Raine, I bought the tickets because I wanted you to fly, as free as a bird. You are not obligated to take me along. They're yours. Do whatever you like with them. Take someone else. Or go by yourself. Whatever you want to do."

He walked to the rocker but didn't touch her. Looking down into her eyes, he added, "And I'd be a liar if I told you I don't want to see you in this teddy. And out of it."

Wanted to see her? Ached would better describe the way he felt. An ache that started in his chest and ended a few feet above his knees. "But not out of obligation. Never out of obligation." Mitch ground the words out then strode away, toward the stairs.

He picked Joey up then turned to face her. How could he make her realize she could love him yet still be free? "Enjoy the ride. I want to hear all about it when you come back down to earth."

The door slammed with a ring of finality, and Raine felt as if she deserved the slam. Feeling guilty, she wandered over to the sofa and stood peering at Mitch's gifts. She took the balloon ride tickets in one hand, the teddy in the other.

Mitch knew her so well, knew she'd love to float in a balloon. And he hadn't imagined her reaction to him. So why had she overreacted?

The antique mantel clock, the one that had belonged to her parents, chimed the quarter hour. She wondered what her mother would say to her, and suddenly wished her parents were alive, wished with all her heart that she could turn to someone for support. There was so much to deal with, so many decisions to make concerning Holly. Clay would have to be told, so would Jeff, the father of Holly's unborn child. Holly didn't have any answers, only more questions. Raine had never seen her sister this way, and had never felt more helpless. Holly alternately pushed Raine away, and cried for help. Raine couldn't tell her what to do, could only be there for her, no matter which decision Holly reached.

Holly's problem wasn't the only thing weighing Raine down. She dreaded going to work more and more each day. Sitting behind a computer hours on end had her climbing the walls. Her car still wasn't running. She'd have to call the garage first thing tomorrow morning. Her refrigerator was empty. The house was a mess, the laundry unfinished.

And she'd hurt Mitch.

He was the one person in the entire world who gave to her. With no strings attached. She didn't know how to take, not from Mitch or from anyone else. She didn't know where this

relationship with him was going. She remembered standing
in the back of his brother's truck the day they'd gone to the
estate sale. He'd said relationships were two-way streets.
Raine rubbed the slinky fabric between her fingers and
thought about one of his rules. *Easygoing people go with
the flow.*

Go with the flow. She wanted to go with the flow. She also
wanted to feel his touch through the satin fabric of the exquisite teddy she held in her hands. She wanted to float up
to the clouds with him, wanted to kiss the sexy smile off his
lips. Then she wanted to put it there again.

Raine suddenly realized what was different about Mitch.
She knew she had a full life, one filled with wonderful people, her family and friends, people who wanted her, truly
needed her. Mitch was different. He wanted her, made no
excuses or denials. But he wouldn't take from her, not until
she took from him, as well.

If Holly decided to keep her baby, she was going to need
all Raine's support. Responsibility hovered on the horizon.
But that was seven months away. Fingering the soft fabric
in her hands, Raine realized she had time to let go, time to
float to the clouds with Mitch. First, she had to convince
him to come along, convince him to share her freedom, if
only for an hour, a day, or a week. She only hoped she'd be
able to find her way out of the clouds when it was all over.

Later that night, Raine decided finding her way out of the
clouds was going to be a lot easier than convincing Mitch she
didn't really feel obligated to him, after all. She'd called to
thank him for the gifts and invited him to come along with
her in the balloon. He'd said *you're welcome,* then politely
refused.

She'd asked him again when she'd called to beg a ride to
work the following morning. His refusal had been even
more adamant when he'd dropped her at the office a few

minutes after eight-thirty. For such a relaxed guy, he was proving to be awfully stubborn.

On Thursday, Raine was contemplating her next course of action concerning Mitch when the phone on her desk rang. Everyone else in the office had gone home an hour ago, and Raine hoped whoever was on the phone wouldn't detain her too much longer. She was tired, she was hungry, she was fidgety.

"Raine? This is Tammy Hart. I tried calling you at home, then took a chance you'd still be at the office."

"What is it, Tammy?" Raine asked, sensing the tension in her friend's voice.

"It's nothing serious. It's just that Robert's out of town and the baby's sick. I have a six forty-five appointment at the pediatrician's, but Mitch hasn't come for Joey. I can't reach him at the office and, since yours is the only name on Joey's emergency form, I was wondering . . ."

"I'll be right over," Raine promised, already reaching for her purse and pressing the proper keys to back up the day's information on the computer.

Fifteen minutes later, she stood in front of the Hart's Day Care sign and waved goodbye to Tammy and her children, who had slightly better than a snowball's chance in July of arriving for their appointment on time. Joey ran ahead of her into Tammy's house, plucked a book off a low table and practically threw it into Raine's hands.

Raine sank onto the sofa, ignoring her rumbling stomach, and smiled when Joey climbed onto her lap. He snuggled into her, pointing to the pictures as she read. The story was about a little white-haired lady who baked cookies for all the neighborhood children, and was obviously one of Joey's favorites.

"Grandma Eva," he said, pointing at a colorful picture.

"Grandma Eva," Raine replied.

The little boy turned his big blue eyes, eyes so like his father's, to hers. "Grandma cry."

Raine's heart rose to her throat at Joey's words. She wondered what the child was thinking, wondered how much of his grandmother he remembered. She wondered if he missed his mother, too, and pressed her lips to his forehead.

"Grandma come see Joey."

"Do you wish your grandmother would come to visit you?" Raine asked.

"Grandma come see Joey. Monday."

She doubted the little boy had any concept of when Monday was. But it was obvious he wanted to see his grandmother again. Did Mitch have any idea of his child's feelings?

She was reading the last page, the third time around, when the door opened and Mitch walked in. Joey didn't scamper off her lap at the first sight of his father as she'd expected. Raine closed the book, the movement causing Joey's head to fall against her arm, and she understood why he hadn't moved. He was sound asleep.

"The little slugger must have fought his nap again today," Mitch whispered, the sight of his son in Raine's arms making it almost impossible to speak. "Where's Tammy?"

"She had to take the baby to the doctor. All the other children had gone for the day. She couldn't reach you, so she called me."

Mitch squared his jaw. Of course. Have a problem, call Raine McAlister. He slid his hand into his pocket to hide his clenched fist. He was angry. Thoroughly ticked off. And hell, he was as guilty of using her as everyone else.

"Thanks, Raine," he said, in what he hoped was a casual tone. "I had a new phone system installed in the offices today. It took a while to get all the kinks worked out of them." It would take a lot longer than an afternoon to remove from his mind the image of Joey's little head nestled next to Raine's breast. He bent to take Joey from her, being careful not to touch where he was looking.

At the door, her voice drew his gaze. "Mitch, there's something I think you should know. Joey thinks his grandmother is coming to see him. On Monday."

"She is."

"She is? Oh."

"Eva's been calling every night. She misses Joey terribly. I didn't know what to do about it. She's his grandmother. She helped Elizabeth raise Joey for two years."

He glanced from the sleeping child in his arms to Raine's face, and sucked in a quick breath. She was looking at him with such an incredibly soft expression, and his mind turned to Saturday night when she'd looked at him in much the same way, when she'd led him up those stairs. He remembered the way she'd felt in his arms, the way she'd clung to him in passion.

"You're a very special man." She smiled, her softest, most beautiful smile, then slowly, so slowly, reached up and feathered a kiss across his mouth. Spellbound, Mitch closed his eyes, and felt an inexplicable sense of rightness at the contact.

She told him goodbye, and propelled him through the door, quietly locking it behind them both before climbing into her small car. He somehow managed to get Joey into his car seat, and drive home, no small feat considering the state his emotions were in.

He used to think roller coasters turned him upside down, leaving his stomach behind. Roller coasters didn't even come close to what Raine did to him with one touch, one smile, one tiny kiss. He'd always loved amusement parks, loved jumping off at the end of a ride and getting back in line again without giving his equilibrium a chance to right itself.

Raine's life was like that line, long and varied, filled with people who needed her, who loved her, who wanted her. This time, Mitch didn't want to stand in line.

* * *

Her birthday dawned unseasonably warm and clear. It was a glorious mid-October day, perfect for taking a balloon ride over the Poconos. Raine stepped out of the shower singing "Happy Birthday" to herself.

She knew what Mitch was doing. He was stubbornly refusing to go on her balloon ride because he wanted her to know she was free. He'd proven his point. Today she was going to ask him again. Today she wasn't taking no for an answer.

She smoothed the teddy up, over her body, humming the birthday song. Mitch had great taste in lingerie. The thin fabric covered her, but didn't conceal. The material was as smooth as satin, and as soft as a whisper. With a smile of anticipation, Raine had a feeling her twenty-ninth birthday was going to be better than any one before.

An hour later, she pressed her finger to Mitch's doorbell. Tanner's anxious barks echoed from inside. After what seemed like several minutes, Mitch opened the door. "Good morning," he said, as if he were testing the idea that it could possibly be a good morning.

"Come with me."

He leaned his hip against the doorframe and crossed first his arms and then his ankles. "Where are you going?"

"Into the wild blue yonder. With you."

He was already shaking his head before she'd uttered the last syllable. That was okay. She hadn't expected him to make it easy. Raine ducked past him into his home. She leaned down to pat Tanner's head, saying, "Tanner, why didn't you tell me your master was this stubborn?"

She turned to Mitch and without missing a beat, said, "Honestly, I want you to go. I'm sorry about the other night. I overreacted. I know this is completely spontaneous and maddeningly presumptuous..."

"Raine, those tickets are yours. You don't have to take me along."

"That's exactly why I want to."

"What?" he asked absently.

"I want you to come with me because I don't have to take you. Because you never expect anything from me, I want to give you this. For my birthday, I want to give you a ride in my balloon."

He didn't say anything, just stood there, staring into her eyes. She didn't know what he was thinking, didn't know what else to say to convince him she *wanted* him to come with her. Except one small word. "Please?"

He didn't move, didn't make a sound. Something deep and primitive passed between them. After what seemed like an eternity, his lips lifted.

That smile of his confused her, sent her pulse racing. "*Easygoing people go with the flow.* You said so yourself."

"So I did."

She watched as Mitch disappeared down the hall. She was still standing in the same position when he returned a few moments later. He rummaged in a drawer then scooped a jacket off the back of the sofa. "Now, where did I put my keys? Taylor stopped in this morning for a game of one-on-one."

"Your keys?" she murmured.

"There they are." He slid them into his pocket.

"What are you doing?" she asked when he picked up the phone.

"Didn't you invite me to ride in your balloon?" Cradling the phone to his ear, Mitch opened the sliding glass door and coaxed Tanner into the fenced-in yard where Joey was playing.

Mitch was usually the one trying to follow the conversation. Raine suddenly understood how it felt to try to muddle through unconnected topics. "Mrs. Tornelli," Mitch said. "Could Jennifer watch Joey this morning? Uh-huh. Right away."

As Raine followed Mitch out his front door ten minutes later, she wondered how he'd ever gotten the upper hand.

* * *

The balloon was nearly flat, lying limp on the ground. Raine handed her certificates to a stockily built man wearing a royal blue coverall. Five other people wearing identical colors were looking on as the huge balloon gradually filled with air.

She and Mitch and the pilot were helped into the basket, which rested on its side. The pilot turned up the burner and, as the balloon filled with hot air, it began to rise, like a sluggish monster coming out of a deep sleep. As the basket was pulled upright, the ground crew steadied it from a rope at each corner. Raine stood at the edge of the basket, which came to her ribs, excitement expanding her chest like the invisible air filling the balloon.

"It's a perfect day for a balloon ride," the pilot informed her. "Just enough breeze to move us along. It'll be a smooth ride."

"How high do you take it?" Mitch asked.

"As high as y'all want to go," the man replied.

"Do you have a license to fly this thing?" Mitch queried.

"In the United States, a pilot must be licensed by the Federal Aviation Administration. I've been piloting balloons for fifteen years. Haven't lost a passenger yet, and don't aim to start today."

"Airplanes are one thing," he grumbled, "but there isn't much to this balloon."

Leaning close, Raine murmured, "Easygoing people don't let a little thing like that spoil their fun."

"I think I've created a monster," he whispered in her ear. She snuggled into his side and, grasping the rim of the basket with one hand, kneaded the taut muscles in Mitch's back with the fingers of the other.

Standing in that flimsy basket with Raine, Mitch decided there was no place in the world he'd rather be. He twined his fingers into her hair, playing with the strands at her nape before gliding his palm down her back. The fabric of her high-necked shirt didn't shimmer over her bare skin, but against another layer, as soft and smooth as satin.

Her eyes were on the ground crew who were unfastening the ropes, but her senses were filled with Mitch. Raine was certain if it wasn't for the whirring sound coming from the burner, everyone within twelve feet would hear the beating of her heart.

The basket lifted from the ground, yet she felt no sensation of losing her stomach. The only indication that they were rising was the brightly clad crew growing steadily smaller down below. The pilot continued to feed fuel to the burner, and the balloon continued to climb toward the clouds.

"You're wearing my gift," Mitch murmured.

She raised her eyes to his. Funny how a little scrap of material could change the way she felt about her appearance. The navy slacks and white top looked exactly as they always had. But underneath, she felt different, provocative, sensuous, almost beautiful.

"How's your stomach?" she asked.

"My stomach?" he repeated absently. "My stomach's all right. But there's one particular area lower than my stomach that's throbbing for attention."

Her reaction to his voice was swift, the thin fabric of the teddy and shirt doing little to hide her taut nipples. She stared open-eyed at his face as his gaze traveled to her breasts. In a voice somewhere between a growl and a whisper, he said, "This is going to be one helluva long trip."

Her laughter rippled through the silence. "Aren't you glad I insisted you come along?"

"I wouldn't miss this for the world."

Raine closed her eyes at his words. Neither would she.

For a moment she'd forgotten they weren't alone. The pilot's southern drawl reminded her of his presence. "The wind is taking us in a north to northeast direction. If it was blowing from the opposite direction, we'd float toward Philadelphia.''

With absolutely no sensation of movement, she felt suspended in thin air while the world flowed away beneath them. As the balloon skimmed over the outskirts of town, the pilot fed more fuel to the burner, raising the balloon to a higher altitude.

''That would be the Interstate,'' the pilot declared, pointing to the ribbon of highway below.

The breeze picked up, so that the ground seemed to sweep along at a faster pace. Raine had never seen trees of crimson and gold from this perspective. Their colors, brightened by the sun's rays, glided away beneath them. ''This must be what they mean by *flying colors,*'' she whispered.

She raised her gaze from the scenery to Mitch's eyes, and was filled with inner excitement. She didn't think a man, any man, could look more ravenous. He didn't attempt to hide his desire and it only fueled her own longings.

''Look, up ahead,'' the pilot instructed.

Raine and Mitch both turned their heads. The countryside was threaded with highways, dotted with trees of magnificent colors, glinted with sunshine. The Pocono Mountains rolled to the west, the Delaware River flowed to the north.

Never before had she seen anything so resplendent. And through that haze of splendor, Raine was totally aware of Mitch. They had separated so that their only connection was their entwined fingers. He brushed half circles on her wrist with his thumb, and her pulse quickened in answer to his touch.

''There's the Delaware Water Gap,'' the pilot persisted, oblivious to the pair making love with their eyes. ''Waters from melting glaciers carried huge quantities of rock and debris through that point in the mountain range millions of years ago. Takes your breath away, doesn't it?''

Raine's cheeks warmed beneath Mitch's gaze. The view hadn't taken her breath away. Mitch had.

"I hope you're enjoying this," Mitch whispered.

"Like a dream," she answered.

"The Delaware River winds along the eastern border of Pennsylvania," the pilot continued. "Just ahead you'll see a railroad bridge that crosses the river. I'm going to land just beyond the next bend."

They floated over the bridge, then gradually began to lose altitude. The descent was just as smooth as the rising had been. The ground crew suddenly appeared down below, waiting to secure the balloon when it landed. With a soft thud, the trip was over. The balloon ride had been wonderful. It was something she'd wanted to see, to experience, all her life, but Raine had never been more ready for something wonderful to end. For now she was filled, was completely consumed, with another kind of wanting.

Chapter Seven

Raine and Mitch stepped from the balloon's basket and thanked the pilot and his crew for the wonderful ride. They'd barely climbed into the back seat of a crew member's Blazer before the man started up a one-sided conversation, a conversation he kept up all the way to Allentown.

Mitch stretched his right arm along the back of the seat behind Raine. The fingers on his other hand trailed across his leg to hers, lazily making figure-eight patterns on the inside of her knee, then moving slightly higher.

"How has your birthday been so far?" he whispered in her ear. For such an innocent question, his deep voice glided over the words, sending anticipation shimmering over her.

"You know it's been wonderful."

His gaze was on her, on the smile playing along the edges of her mouth. She looked into his eyes, watching his eyes travel over her face. The very air surrounding them seemed filled with waiting. She breathed that air into her lungs, and the sense of what was to come filled her with longing. When the driver turned onto the lane where they'd begun their balloon ride, she and Mitch exchanged a private look. Her emotions whirled, her senses reeled.

Alone in his car moments later, she took his hand in hers, dreamily whispering, "I'm twenty-nine years old today, and this has been the most incredible birthday I've ever had. That balloon ride was more wonderful than I imagined, and if I live to be a hundred and twenty-nine, I'll still look back to this birthday and remember you."

Her words had a sobering effect on him. They reminded him that she wasn't planning her future around him. She wasn't even planning it with him. He knew she wanted him, but he also knew she wanted to be free. She still didn't realize she could have both. Mitch was beginning to worry that she never would.

He gazed into her eyes for interminable seconds, trying to read her thoughts. He'd never felt quite this way, had never felt so close to another human being. Words of love spun through his mind. Uncertainty kept them from his lips.

He started his car without releasing her hand. Before putting the lever into drive, he pulled her close and kissed her the way he'd wanted to all day. Raine closed her eyes and kissed him back, and Mitch wondered how he was ever going to convince her their lives belonged together.

"Oh, Mitch," she whispered. "I feel like this is all an adventure, and you're the biggest adventure of all."

The car's tires churned over the loose gravel, and Mitch's thoughts churned through his mind. There had been a time when hearing such words would have made him feel incredibly smug. Not anymore. He knew, from the way she'd kissed him, from the way she'd looked at him and touched him, she was ready for their relationship to deepen. His desire for her was pulsing through him, but he wanted more than a physical relationship with Raine.

She'd told him, from the very beginning, that she didn't want commitment. She'd been honest, and he knew she cared for him, just as she cared for all the people in her life.

She also desired him, but Mitch was afraid that if he took her to bed now, it would be all they'd ever have. She'd view their relationship as an idyllic interlude, as an affair. When it was over, she'd go on with the rest of her life... without him.

A cold shower wouldn't have had this much effect on his desire. Oh, no, he wasn't going to give in to this attraction. Not until she knew it was more than physical.

Mitch was going to have to think fast, to come up with a plan, one that would make her want him more than she'd ever wanted anyone before. He needed time, and so did Raine. Time to date him, time to know him, time to grow to love him. He needed to find ways to be together, so she'd have time to do all those things, and Mitch decided that lunch was a good place to start.

"Where would you like to eat lunch?" he asked.

"Lunch?"

"Yeah. It's your birthday. You get to choose. Rule number forty-three."

"I thought we'd go back to my place," she said softly.

Mitch closed his eyes and tried to tramp down the images floating across his imagination. "I'd love to go back to your place, Raine," he said. "But I'm afraid Jennifer can't stay all day." That was true enough. Jennifer couldn't watch Joey all day, but she could have watched him for a few more hours. She could have watched him while he and Raine went back to her place and made love.

That's exactly what Mitch wanted to do. He wanted to make love with Raine until she came to her senses and realized she loved him and wanted to spend the rest of her life with him. But Mitch didn't want to be a one-night stand, and she wasn't ready to make a lasting commitment. There was too much at stake to risk losing her now.

"Oh," she murmured.

"Believe me, Raine," he declared. "I want you. But when we do finally go to bed, I want to make it last." *About fifty years, at least,* he added to himself.

He saw her expression soften, saw her slow smile. She was thinking about making love, and it was all Mitch could do to keep from turning the car around and heading straight for her place.

"You want me to choose the restaurant?" she asked. "Any place they serve cheeseburgers and chocolate shakes. I don't know if I can look at another microwave dinner as long as I live."

A short time later, Raine sat across from Mitch, sipping her shake and laughing as he regaled her with stories of his brothers, of the sometimes funny, sometimes embarrassing situations they'd found themselves in over the years. His eyes twinkled with devilment, and she doubted she'd ever forget a single detail of this day. Her birthday hadn't turned out exactly as she'd planned, but she'd never felt so alive, or so lighthearted.

The restaurant was far from quiet. It was a weekend, after all, yet Raine was oblivious to everyone else. She fed their used napkins and wrappers to the trash container, her mind spinning with images of his tales. She was so engrossed in Mitch, she wouldn't have noticed the woman entering if she hadn't nearly collided with her on the way out the door.

"Hi, Raine!" the woman said.

"Clarissa!" Raine returned. Her gaze strayed to a dark haired child at Clarissa's side who walked with the aid of crutches. "Who's this?" Raine asked.

"I'm Stephanie," the little girl answered.

"My daughter," Clarissa added.

Stephanie looked fragile in her leg braces and crutches, her eyes too large for her face. Clarissa hadn't mentioned her daughter's defect when she'd bumped into her a few weeks ago. Raine wondered why. Remembering her manners, she said, "This is Mitch Harris. He's just treated me to a birthday lunch."

"Mommy, I'm hungry," the little girl declared.

Clarissa smiled at her daughter, but Raine noticed the line that had formed between her old friend's eyes. Clarissa had something on her mind.

"Raine, could you meet me for lunch on Monday?"

"Of course."

Clarissa hurried away, then turned, and over her shoulder, named a time and place. Mitch watched her go, and swore under his breath. He hadn't missed the worry in the other woman's expression. Raine was about to be dumped on again.

"Clarissa. Wasn't she one of the single friends you were going to introduce to me?" Mitch asked.

"Yes," Raine answered. "Don't be offended, but I'm afraid Clarissa isn't interested in dating. Not even you."

Not even you. Her words bolstered his confidence. Raine, at least, thought he was something special. He supposed that was a start. The problem was, Mitch was getting tired of starts. He was ready for more, a lot more, a lifetime more.

In his car moments later, he tried to think of some way to warn her about becoming involved in other people's problems. It was one of the things he admired about her, and one of the things that infuriated him the most.

He felt the world intruding on them, and wanted to turn back the clock to a few hours ago, when there was nothing but the two of them and a hot air balloon, no worries, no insecurities.

"Just look at the time." He heard the smile in her voice, now mellow and relaxed. "I never used to be late for anything."

He smiled, momentarily forgetting his worries. She hadn't jiggled her foot all day. Maybe she'd stop allowing the people she loved to heap their problems on her, too.

"What are you late for?" he asked.

"Holly and Clay are coming over later and I still have to frost my birthday cake."

"You baked your own birthday cake?"

"I always do."

He pulled into his driveway and parked next to her car. Why couldn't she see the way her brother and sister, and nearly everyone else, walked all over her? He clenched his jaw and tapped his fingers on the steering wheel in an effort to keep from saying what was on his mind.

"Holly's going to tell Clay about the baby, and I want to be there if they need me." She squeezed his arm and reached up to graze his mouth with a kiss. Regrets assailed him. What right did he have to be angry because she chose to live her life in her own way?

Slowly, she reached her hand to his cheek, pressing her palm to his clenched jaw. "Thanks for today, Mitch. It's been more like an adventure than a birthday, and it's all because of you."

He took her hand, suddenly reluctant to let her go. Pressing his mouth to hers, he felt her lips part, heard her murmur of surprise. "Want to come inside for a few minutes?"

Mitch saw the surprise in her eyes, and saw her glance at her watch. She nodded, even though he knew she hadn't expected his simple request. For a change, he'd been the one to catch *her* off guard, and Mitch felt a portion of his old self-confidence return.

Mitch casually took her hand in his, and just as casually sauntered into the house. He nonchalantly paid Jennifer, who'd told him Joey had been sleeping for the past two hours. His casual attitude disappeared the moment Jennifer walked out the door.

Still holding Raine's hand, he kicked the front door shut, then pressed Raine's back against the wall, fitting his body to hers. She buried her hands in his thick hair, pulling his face to hers. The woman kissed like a dream, and Mitch felt a response deep in his body. But he had no intention of letting this go too far.

The muffled yap of a dog drew their gazes to the sliding glass door. Tanner sat on the deck, his brown eyes eager, his tail wagging with total abandon. "Tanner wants to come inside," Raine whispered.

Mitch wanted the same thing, but closed his eyes against what he wanted to say. He moved his lips over her temple, down her cheekbone, along her jaw, making no move to open the door for his dog.

"He thinks he's your best friend."

"Believe me," he answered. "He understands. Whenever he sees the cute little poodle across the street, Tanner forgets I'm even alive."

Raine smiled, and once again felt as if she were floating. Since the moment she'd laid eyes on Mitch this morning, he'd done nothing she'd expected. He'd agreed to go with her in the balloon when she'd expected him to adamantly refuse. Afterward, he'd taken her to lunch, when she'd expected him to go with her to her house. He'd casually taken her hand and led her inside his house, then kissed her in anything but a casual way.

They both knew Joey was due to wake up any minute, but Mitch was looking at her as if he wanted to lead her down the short hall, straight to his bedroom. For a moment, he gazed at her with so much feeling she couldn't move. Desire deepened his breathing, invitation darkened the blue of his eyes. She'd thought he'd open the door for Tanner. Instead, he ran his hands along her shoulders, down her arms and back up again. She heard his sharp intake of breath as he smoothed his palms down her back, and knew he felt the satin teddy underneath.

His fingers dipped inside the waistband of her navy slacks, and she felt the deft movements of his fingertips. She'd wondered if he'd make love with the same lazy single-mindedness he did everything else. But there was nothing lazy about the way he was touching her.

Raine trailed kisses down his neck, then stepped back to look into his eyes. Mitch seemed to withstand her look as long as he could before pulling her against him, his voice a husky murmur as he promised, "Keep looking at me like that and I won't be held accountable for my actions."

She felt drawn to Mitch much the way she felt drawn to high places, and beautiful views. "I know what it's like to be held accountable for others, Mitch. Believe me, I'm not asking that of you."

The faint tremor in her voice told him more than her words. Mitch searched her face, reaching into her thoughts. Day by day, he was beginning to understand her need for freedom. Day by day, he wanted her more. He figured it was a good thing Joey was due to wake up any minute. Otherwise, he might not have been able to keep himself from touching her again.

He opened the sliding door for his dog, then hunkered down, scratching Tanner's head. Raine went down to her knees, too. Joey chose that moment to wake up and call for his father. Raine tipped her head to one side, saying, "Would you like me to get him for you?"

Mitch ran his hand along hers, but kept his touch light. "No, Raine. I don't want you to do anything you don't want to do. This is your special day, and I want you to be completely carefree."

Raine felt tears sting her eyes, and she hardly ever cried. Mitch brought her emotions to the surface. He was a very special man. She doubted he knew just how special he really was. "What if I told you I wanted to?"

He squeezed her hand. "All right. If you *want* to, be my guest. I'm sure Joey will be happy to see you."

Raine rose and Mitch watched as she turned away. With a style and grace that was hers alone, she flitted down the hall toward Joey's room. Mitch stayed where he was, unable to get the look he'd seen deep in her eyes out of his mind.

He took a steak bone from the refrigerator. After unwrapping it, he offered it to Tanner, who took it between his teeth, and with toenails clicking over the linoleum, plopped down underneath the table to chew to his heart's content.

From inside the kitchen, Mitch heard a drawer squeak open in Joey's room, heard Raine talking to his son. There was a softness in her voice, a special degree of caring Mitch could hear from here. Emotions welled up all the way to the center of him, feelings for his child, and for the woman with the soft voice and honest smile.

Mitch heard Joey's laughter, and moments later, the slap-slap of his small feet as he ran ahead of Raine into the kitchen. He remembered how he'd felt that first day with Joey, how inadequate and unsure he'd been in his abilities to be a good father. Watching Joey now, Mitch felt confidence and pride in his son.

Watching Raine with Joey, Mitch also understood why he loved her. She was caring, and passionate about life, about living. He knew he couldn't force her to love him back, but gazing into her eyes, he sensed she'd already started to care. Maybe, if he was patient and didn't hurry her, that caring would turn into love.

She leaned down to talk to Joey, her movements drawing her blouse closer to her body. He could see a narrow strap through the thin fabric, and followed it's smooth line to her breasts. Raine chose that moment to look up at him, and Mitch felt his patience grow thin.

She didn't smile, but in her expression he saw an incredible sense of composure, and a subtle kind of happiness.

"Gum," Joey said, pulling Raine's oversize purse from the counter.

Raine reached for her purse, but it was too late. It hit the floor with a thud, its contents spilling everywhere. "I don't have any gum, Joey," she murmured, immediately beginning to scoop the articles back into her large bag. Mitch bent to help, picking up lipstick, her wallet, a set of keys.

Both their hands reached for another package, this one small and square and wrapped in foil. Mitch recognized a package of protection when he saw it. The fact that it had been in Raine's purse bolstered his ego. She wanted him. And when she realized she loved him, too, he'd make sure they both got what they wanted.

"Keep this, Raine," he whispered, handing the foil package to her. "I have a feeling we'll be using it."

"Pretty sure of yourself," she replied.

"Should I be?"

He watched her hand close around the package, watched as she placed it inside her purse. Her eyes told him things she hadn't said. She glanced at her watch, and back at the package in her hand, whispering, "I wish Holly would have used one of these, Mitch. She's barely nineteen years old. I still have to remind her to make her bed. How is she going to be a mother?"

Mitch didn't know what to say. The world had a way of intruding, and there wasn't a thing he could do about it.

Raine called goodbye to Joey, and Mitch squeezed her hand in his, conveying in the firm pressure of his fingers that she wasn't really alone. She settled the strap of her purse on her shoulder, and slipped through his front door. From the window, Mitch and Joey watched her turn to wave from the driveway. Mitch raised his own hand, and smiled back at her. The smile felt wooden, and pulled at the muscles in his clenched jaw.

"Me hungry, Daddy."

Heaving a deep sigh, Mitch set about preparing a grilled cheese sandwich, Joey's *goodest* food this week, then sat down near his son to watch him eat. The towheaded boy was in one of his more angelic moods, taking a bite of his sandwich, then holding it up for Mitch. "Daddy take bite."

Mitch's heart rose to his throat each time Joey said *daddy*. Had it really been only a little over a month since he'd learned he even had a son? He took a bite of the sandwich and playfully nibbled Joey's chubby finger in the process. Joey giggled, and pressed his little hand to his father's cheek. Raine had done the same thing, pressed her palm to his jaw in a comforting gesture.

Mitch didn't feel comforted. What he felt was frustration. He wanted Raine, in his life, in every way possible.

After loading the dishwasher after supper, he plunked Joey into the tub for the boy's bath. He washed his son's hair and scrubbed his little body as if he'd been doing it all his life. Mitch remembered when Raine had shown him how. She'd told him it would all be as natural to him as breathing in a matter of a few short weeks. She'd been right.

At eight, he tucked Joey into bed, along with his tattered blanket and three favorite stuffed animals, a bear from his Grandpa and Grandma Harris, an elephant from Uncle Taylor and the black puppy he'd received from Raine and called Toto-From-Kansas.

He pulled the shades and turned off the lamp, then tucked the sheet under Joey's chin. "Night-night, Daddy," Joey mumbled around his thumb.

"Night, slugger." Mitch knew there'd be hell to pay in orthodontist's fees later from Joey's thumb-sucking. But for now, there wasn't a lot he could do about it.

He stopped in the doorway of his own bedroom, looking at the rumpled comforter and the pillow where he and Raine could have made love. Exotic images swirled through his mind, images of how she'd look in that teddy, and how she'd look out of it. He remembered the night he'd given it to her, remembered how she'd reacted. She'd said the teddy was like a rope anchoring her balloon to the ground. That scrap of material wasn't her anchor. All the people who heaped their problems on her shoulders kept her from her dreams.

Mitch strode to the deck where Tanner dropped his favorite ball at Mitch's feet and waited for him to toss it. He scooped the ball up and threw it to the edge of his yard, but his heart wasn't really in the game. He didn't know where his heart was. It didn't feel the way it was supposed to.

Raine thought of him as one of her adventures. But he didn't want to be just another adventure, here this week, gone the next. He wanted to be *the* adventure. One that lasted forever.

Tanner came bounding back with the rubber ball and dropped it on the deck, his tail wagging, waiting for his due praise. Mitch absently rubbed the length of Tanner's back. "I think I know how you feel when that cute poodle with the little bow on one ear will have nothing to do with you."

Tanner answered with a loud thump of his tail.

Loving Raine had reduced him to this. Mitch was about to pour his heart out to a dog, and Tanner wasn't even a purebred.

"An adventure. She considers me an adventure. She's the one who insists on flying. But I'm the one who has to come back down to earth, again and again."

Mitch's doorbell sounded, stopping his tirade. Tanner barked, two short yips and one low growl. "That'll be Kyle, huh, Tanner?" Mitch strode through the house to the front door.

"You look like something the cat dragged in," Kyle taunted as soon as Mitch opened the door.

"Nice to see you, too."

"Are you in the middle of something important? You and Tanner having fun in the backyard?"

Tanner growled. So did Mitch. "I haven't had this much fun since my last root canal," he answered.

Kyle, who'd never gotten over his wariness of Tanner, or of Joey, for that matter, grumbled, "That dog hates me." He glanced around the interior of Mitch's house and de-

clared, "I thought you were going to clean this place up a
little."

"I have."

"Could have fooled me. Are you really planning to bring
Joey's grandmother here?"

Mitch slid one hand into his pocket, the other through his
hair, hair that was overdue for a good cut and style. "She
loves Joey. She needs to see for herself that he's happy."

"So send her a picture, or put her up in a motel, but have
her stay here? Mitch, are you crazy?"

Mitch didn't claim he wasn't nervous about the arrangement. He'd only spent one night with Joey's mother. How
was he going to get through an entire week with Joey's
grandmother? For all he knew, Eva hated him for getting
her daughter in trouble, although Mitch hadn't known
about the baby. And then there was this problem with
Raine. She was the woman he wanted to see, the woman he
wanted to spend the week with.

It took Mitch a few moments to realize Kyle was talking.
He caught enough of his brother's words to know Kyle was
asking about their latest bet. "I think Taylor's full of hot
air. I don't think he's dating anyone, let alone a woman with
three kids. I wouldn't be surprised if he shows up at the
folks' party stag. How about you?"

Mitch still hadn't told either of his brothers about Raine.
What was there to tell? Not that that had ever stopped him
from bragging in the past. He'd recounted tales of women
he'd known a lot less intimately than Raine. But that was
different. What he felt for Raine was different. He only
hoped what she felt for him in return was half as special to
her.

Maybe Raine wasn't proclaiming her undying love. Mitch
grimaced at that understatement. But then, she'd as much
as admitted that she wanted him, at least physically, and
there wasn't a lot he could do about the rest, at least not at

the moment. He slid his hand into his pocket and rattled his loose change.

"Come on, Kyle. Let's play some ball."

"Again? Didn't you and Taylor already burn up the pavement this morning?"

Mitch didn't bother answering. He grabbed the ball and headed for the hoop in the driveway. Maybe a good game of basketball was just what he needed. Maybe, after some intense physical exertion, he'd be able to come up with a new plan. Maybe then, he'd decide what he should do about Raine and this relationship she looked on as nothing more than a big adventure.

Maybe then, he'd know how to tell her he was in love with her, without scaring her away.

Chapter Eight

Smiling into the darkness in her bedroom, Raine fluffed up her pillow, pulling the sheet and blanket over her shoulders. She couldn't remember enjoying a birthday so thoroughly, not even as a child. According to the dial on her clock radio, she still had seventeen minutes before her special day was over, and she wanted to savor every last second.

She'd been happy since the moment she'd opened her eyes, and that happiness had only intensified in the hours since. Memories of the balloon ride with Mitch floated through her mind. The scenery alone would have been enough to cheer about, and the sensation of soaring had been out of this world. To experience such a ride would have been enough to keep her smiling all day; to experience the kind of passion she'd found in Mitch's kiss a short time later might just keep her smiling all week.

Raine rolled to her side and closed her eyes as she thought about Holly and Clay. They'd both come home from Philadelphia because it was her birthday. When Holly told Clay about her pregnancy, Raine's birthday had been forgotten. But they'd all been together, and she felt the rightness of it even now.

Poor Clay. He'd been furious and had wanted to drag Jeff off by the throat, although that wasn't exactly the terminology her brother had used. Holly had surprised them both when she'd defended Jeff, when she told them she loved him. Raine shouldn't have been surprised. She hadn't raised Holly these past ten years to take matters of the heart lightly. Of course she'd be in love with the young man who'd fathered her child.

"Then maybe you should marry him!" Clay had sputtered.

Holly's eyes had taken on a dreamy look. "Maybe I will."

The conversation had run in spirals after that, as they discussed Holly's alternatives, how she felt, what she wanted. For the first time, Raine had noticed her brother and sister had grown up. It was the first time they'd tackled a major problem together, almost equally. Although they still looked to their older sister for guidance and comfort, and she was still concerned about Holly's age and impending motherhood, Raine couldn't help but feel a swelling pride in her brother and sister. They really had grown up.

She yawned and her eyes fluttered closed again. Her birthday was officially over. Raine remembered how she'd anticipated spending it with Mitch. She'd thought it was going to be better than any other, and she'd been right. She'd assumed part of the reason would be because she and Mitch would make love. They hadn't, but it didn't detract from her newly awakened sense of freedom.

On impulse, she switched on the lamp and dialed Mitch's number. Halfway through the third ring, she heard a muffled thud. Moments later, Mitch's low voice rumbled a husky greeting.

"Were you sleeping?" Raine asked in a soft voice.

"That depends. Am I dreaming?"

His words caused her eyelids to lower. He had her upside down, and he was too sleepy to know it. She wanted him. She had from the first moment she saw him. He wanted her, too. Some things were impossible to disguise. Raine had never felt more breathless with anticipation.

"You're not dreaming, Mitch. I just called to say thanks."

"For what?"

"For everything. Now go back to sleep. I'll see you soon." She replaced the receiver and switched off the light, the sound of Mitch's deep voice still echoing through her mind.

She'd never met a man like him, a man so strong, so comfortable with the world, a man who liked her for herself, and who placed no demands on her. Her last waking thoughts swirled into oblivion and she drifted off to sleep.

The following evening, Raine wrapped up her birthday cake and, holding it close to her body to protect it from the autumn wind, placed it on the seat beside her. Clay had taken a look at her car's engine that morning, ran to the store where he bought something or other that needed replacing and had the car running again before he'd left for college that afternoon.

He'd smiled sheepishly when she'd thanked him, and turned an adorable shade of pink when she'd asked who he was hurrying off to see. He hadn't mentioned any names, but Raine had a feeling the woman must be pretty special to have him turning down Raine's applesauce cake.

Holly hadn't wanted any cake, either. Instead of turning pink like her brother, she'd turned a funny shade of green at the mere mention of anything sweet. She'd taken a handful of saltines, instead, and caught a ride back to school with Clay and his friend. Raine had waved goodbye from the back step. On her way past the laundry room, she noticed

Holly's cream knit dress, on which she found a note. *Rainie, would you wash this for me? Please?*

Some things changed, but others never would.

With the wind whipping her hair into her eyes, it was all Raine could do to find her way to Mitch's a few minutes later. The door opened before she'd rung the bell, and she'd hardly taken two steps inside before Mitch's mouth covered hers. He kissed her urgently, and she reacted with a sense of abandon all her own.

Raising her mouth from his, Raine shifted the cake to one hand and pushed the hair from her eyes. She laughed and took her first good look at him. "Hello, Mitch. I thought that was you."

"What would it take to make you sure?"

Raine was enthralled by the seduction in his voice. His smile held a glimmer of eroticism, and his eyes, which were nearly the same color as the sky outside, would have betrayed his ardor even without that kiss. Her heart expanded and her pulse pounded. Her mind spun and her lips instinctively found their way to his once more.

With the cake held between them, their mouths were the only place they touched. Raine couldn't ignore the strange aching in her limbs when their lips parted on a sigh. She looked down at the cake in her hand, and her reason for stopping by. "Clay and Holly and I never got around to cutting into my birthday cake yesterday. And I thought Joey might get a kick out of helping me blow out my candles."

For the first time since she'd arrived, Raine looked around. "Mitch, what happened to your house? I mean, this is *your* house, isn't it?"

Mitch ran his fingers through his freshly cut hair, but didn't readily answer. "Is everything all right?" she asked.

"Sure."

"Where's Joey?"

"He's in the backyard. With Eva."

Understanding dawned. His haircut, his neat and tidy house. It was all beginning to make sense. "I thought you said she wasn't coming until tomorrow."

"That's what I thought, too. She arrived on my doorstep about nine last night. Honestly, Raine, she just showed up, out of the blue, saying how much she appreciated my inviting her and how much she's missed Joey. She decided to surprise us and come a day early."

Raine tried to see the horror in the situation, but ended up seeing the humor, instead. She tried not to laugh, really she did, but without much success. "What did you do?"

"I let her in. And that was about the last thing I've done on my own since."

"You didn't clean the house?" Raine asked.

"Eva did it."

"And your haircut?"

"I figured you'd notice. She sent Joey and I out this afternoon."

"I thought you said she was in failing health."

"I thought she was," Mitch sputtered. "For a seventy-four-year-old widow in poor health, she's as strong as a horse."

Raine laughed, and the sound circled his heart. She carried the cake into the kitchen where she placed it on the counter and looked out the window at Joey and Eva Russell. "So she doesn't remind you of her daughter?"

Mitch waited to answer until she looked up at him and then, he merely shook his head. "I'm afraid I didn't know Elizabeth well enough to know if she'd been like Eva or not." He could barely remember what the other woman had looked like, yet he doubted he'd ever forget the way Raine's eyes looked at that moment.

"How did Elizabeth die?" Raine whispered.

"She had an aneurysm in her brain. Eva said she died instantly."

The glass door slid open and Joey bounded in. With a smile of pure joy at seeing Raine, the little boy ran across the room. Mitch watched Raine go down to her knees to hug his son, and knew with a pulse-pounding certainty that he wanted her in his life. Permanently.

Raine picked Joey up and patted his little bottom. "What's this? No diapers?"

Joey looked into her eyes and sheepishly said, "Me big boy. Wear big-boy pants."

Mitch hadn't wanted to push Joey, had worried he'd suffered enough trauma in his short life, what with losing his mother and meeting his father for the first time and moving a thousand miles across the country. Eva had no such worries. She'd been here less than twenty-four hours and she'd already taken over. She had the house clean, Joey out of diapers and Mitch out of his mind.

"You must be Raine." Eva had watched the affection between Raine and Joey, too. Her shrewd look, along with her words, brought Mitch back to his senses. He handled the introductions, and was relieved when Raine smiled at the older woman. Joey seemed perfectly content to remain in Raine's arms, and frankly, Mitch couldn't blame him.

As the evening progressed, Mitch relaxed. Raine infected the very air he breathed with sunshine. She sang "Happy Birthday" to herself for Joey's benefit and let him help her blow out the candles. She accepted Eva's bluntness as naturally as she accepted everyone else. By the time Raine was preparing to leave at a little after nine, she'd exchanged lasagna recipes with the older woman and listened to Eva's advice on applying tung oil to antique furniture.

Mitch brushed his lips across Raine's at the door, and would have sold his soul for half an hour alone with her. "Have lunch with me tomorrow."

"I can't, Mitch. I'm meeting Clarissa Cohagan."

She called goodbye to Joey, who watched her drive away. Before Raine had pulled out of the driveway, the child started to cry. Joey was overtired and overwrought. Those tears grew into wails, which grew into the first temper tantrum Mitch had witnessed.

By the time Joey had finally dropped off to sleep with a sob and a hiccup half an hour later, Mitch felt wrung out. He still had the entire week to get through with Eva Russell, and he felt no closer to hearing words of love from Raine than he'd been over a month ago.

Something else was beginning to worry him. Joey was becoming attached to Raine.

The next day, Raine arrived at the restaurant only moments ahead of her friend Clarissa. She normally worked through her lunch hour on Mondays so she could leave at four to attend her flight lesson. But Clarissa had looked so serious when she'd asked Raine to lunch, she decided to skip the class just this once. There had been something in her friend's expression she simply couldn't ignore. They'd been close friends all through high school, until Clarissa had moved away nine years ago.

Over the years, they'd lost touch. But sitting across from her today, Raine felt the old bond of friendship resurface. Clarissa wore a two-piece dress of dark blue. Her hair was fastened at her nape, but a shock of coffee-colored tresses waved to one side of her face. Clarissa had always had class, but the past nine years had made her more sure of herself, more subtle and refined.

Raine was sure she hadn't misread the worry in her friend's eyes last Saturday, and she'd expected Clarissa to confide in her now. But if Clarissa did have any problems, she didn't mention them to Raine today. Instead, they just talked. Not as one person who needed the advice and strength of another, but as friends.

Clarissa talked about her daughter, about the apartment they were renting in Quakertown and about her business, which was growing by leaps and bounds. Raine found herself laughing, telling Clarissa about Clay and Holly and her flight lessons. Raine found herself talking candidly, openly about her life, about her house, even about her ever-growing dislike of her job.

Clarissa's eyes had narrowed. After a moment of deliberate thought, she said, "Raine, you said you have experience with computers, and you're the most organized person I've ever met. I've been thinking . . ." she hesitated.

"Clarissa, what is it?" Raine asked.

"How would you feel about becoming my assistant? It would mean you could quit your other job, and as a wedding consultant, your responsibilities would be varied, believe me. I never sit still."

Raine's eyes widened. She'd expected Clarissa to talk about her troubles. Instead, she'd just offered her a new job.

Clarissa answered all Raine's questions about her type of work, and laughed along with her, sharing in her excitement. "I'll have to think about it," Raine said, but she had a feeling Clarissa read the answer in the sparkle in her eyes.

"Clarissa, this is amazing! When Clay and Holly left for college in August, I promised myself freedom. But it hasn't been that easy. My life has been like a ride in a stunt plane these past weeks. When one problem seems insurmountable, something exciting appears from behind a cloud and I find myself soaring toward another adventure."

"Where does Mitch Harris fit in with all this?"

Raine had already mentioned Mitch, but today, she told Clarissa about the first time she saw him, and about the balloon ride she'd taken with him on her birthday. "He's the most self-possessed person I've ever met. Even being thrust into fatherhood didn't rattle him for long. He simply took Joey in stride, proving to be a wonderful caring father, albeit a sloppy one. How many men do you know who wouldn't make any demands in a similar situation?"

"Maybe I'm not the right person to ask about men. I'm afraid I don't have much faith in them, but Raine, are you sure about this? He's a bachelor and has a two-year-old child, yet he wants nothing from you?"

Clarissa's words were sobering. "He doesn't seem to," Raine murmured.

"Haven't you talked about this? I know what it's like to be a single parent. Everything I do affects Stephanie. If Mitch is really the wonderful father you say he is, wouldn't he be concerned his son might become attached to you?"

Raine remembered how Joey's face had lit up when he'd first seen her last night. Clarissa's words held so much wisdom it scared her. *Was* the child becoming too attached to her? *Was* Mitch concerned about it?

Raine and Clarissa changed the subject, and finished their lunch. By the time she'd left the restaurant, Raine was smiling once again. She'd as much as told Clarissa she'd take the job, and couldn't wait to tell Mitch. She'd also promised herself that before their relationship went any further, she'd talk to him about Joey.

"Mitch!" The excitement in Raine's voice vibrated over the telephone wires. He pictured the way her eyes would be twinkling. "Guess what? I have a new job. And I wanted you to be the first to know."

His chair creaked as he leaned back to prop both feet on his desk. It was so good to hear her voice.

"You remember the other day when I ran into Clarissa?"

"Yes..."

"She started her own business five years ago. She said her daughter and her business are both growing too fast for her to keep up. You know, Mitch, I don't think your receptionist approves of my calling you at the office. Anyway, she needs someone to help her."

"My receptionist?"

"No, Clarissa."

Mitch gave up trying to follow the conversation after that. Only Raine could begin talking about her new job, get side-tracked into topics about lunch and a little girl he didn't know, only to end up where she'd started, talking about her new job.

Candace poked her head in the office halfway through Raine's rambling. "Mrs. Parker is here." Mitch nodded to his co-worker who immediately disappeared down the hall.

When Raine stopped to take a breath, he murmured, "I want to hear all about it, Raine, but my next patient just arrived. Why don't you meet me at my place in an hour? We'll celebrate. There's something I want to talk to you about, too."

"There is? What?"

"Not over the phone. We'll talk at my place, unless you'd rather meet at yours."

"Won't Eva be at your place?"

"My parents called, claiming they wanted to get to know Eva, and begging to spend some time with Joey. They picked both Joey and Eva up bright and early this morning and headed back to Philadelphia until tomorrow night. I think Kyle had something to do with all this, but I'm not sure how he managed to pull it off."

By the time he'd finished, Raine was laughing. He told her where he hid his spare key, but now that he had her on the phone, he was reluctant to let her break the connection. After she'd hung up her end, he sat holding the receiver for several seconds.

The past five minutes were the first he'd fully relaxed since she'd driven away the evening of her birthday. Hearing her voice over the phone later that night had only intensified his worries. His heated game of one-on-one with Kyle hadn't resulted in any clear, brilliant plan to win Raine's love. When she'd charmed Eva Russell the following night, when she'd opened her arms to Joey, when she'd kissed *him* with that silly cake between them, then looked into his eyes and laughed, he knew he was lost. He was beginning to understand her need for freedom. He had a similar need for her.

She wanted to take risks, to experience all the adventure she'd missed. He understood about risks—he'd taken one when he became involved with her. Look where that had gotten him. She deserved a little freedom. For her own good, he didn't want to cage her in.

The hell he didn't.

Raine was aware that her foot was jiggling. Mitch wouldn't approve. He'd tell her to relax. He'd probably remind her that easygoing people don't jiggle their feet. That would make her laugh, and laughter would relieve her tension, which was why she was jiggling her foot in the first place.

She stood and wandered around his living room. "The problem with this house is it's all on one floor," she muttered to Tanner. There were no stairs. Everything was within easy reach. Including Mitch. That's what was making her so nervous. The short hall led to his bedroom, and from the open doorway she could hear water spouting from Mitch's shower, bouncing off the tiles and glass doors. In her imagination she saw Mitch, clean-scrubbed, with droplets of water clinging to his body, a body she'd dreamed about three nights in a row.

The water was turned off. The shower door slid open. A moment later, she heard the muffled sound of Mitch's whistle. Her heart hammered, her limbs suddenly felt like softened wax. Raine entertained the idea of marching the few feet to his bedroom, bursting into the shower and kissing that whistle right off his lips. Instead, she wandered aimlessly into his kitchen.

First, she had to talk to him about what was best for Joey. Raine thought about the conversation she'd had with Clarissa, when her friend had asked if she'd talked to Mitch about what he wanted from her. What did he expect? Joey did need a mother. Every child did. How could she explain that even though she wouldn't hurt Joey for the world, she wasn't sure she'd ever be ready for that kind of responsibility?

Mitch deserved to know. He was everything she'd ever dreamed a man should be. She had to be certain he understood.

There hadn't been any sound, yet she knew he'd entered the room behind her. She turned, first her head and then the rest of her body. For a moment, she stood motionless, looking at him across the room, trying to form the proper words. "You're late."

"I know." His blue eyes were compelling. He looked confident, from his broad shoulders all the way down to his bare feet. His shirt was unbuttoned, his faded jeans beltless, his thumbs hooked through two of the loops.

With long strides he crossed the space between them. Her eyes were fixed on his face, where droplets of water still clung to his forehead. She reached up to brush them away, and he covered her hand with his, smoothing her palm over his jaw, down his neck, to the center of his chest. His heart thumped beneath her palm, and her mind turned to the last time she'd touched him.

"Mitch," she whispered. "We have to talk."

He took another step, stopping when a mere inch separated his thighs from hers. She would only have to lean forward to brush against him, to press her breasts to his bare chest.

She ran her tongue over her dry lips, then watched as his eyelids lowered in response. "What did you want to talk about?"

Outwardly, he appeared calm, but the way his heart hammered beneath her palm was anything but. Her own heart rate accelerated and Raine leaned into him. Raising her head to his, she kissed him, savoring the moment.

Her hand was captured between their bodies, between her fluttering heartbeat and his. He slid his left hand around to her back and his thumb followed the narrow dip of her spine. A shudder passed through her, nearly draining away all her doubts and fears.

"Mitch, you know what I want?" she asked, pulling back slightly.

"I have a pretty good idea."

His words made her smile, and she pressed her lips to the thick column of his neck. "You, Mitch Harris, have an attitude."

"So I've been told."

She slid both hands to his chest and peered into his eyes. "I'd be lying if I told you I don't want you." When he began to lower his head to hers, she added, "But first, I have to be completely honest with you."

He straightened and took a deep breath, letting her go by degrees. "All right. If you're going to fill our time with honesty, let's at least get comfortable."

He tugged her hand and walked with her to the living room, where he sat down on the floor with his back against the sofa, crossed his ankles and peered up at her. "Well?"

Raine shook her head. After a moment, she slipped her shoes off and joined him on the carpet. Now that they were side by side, she didn't know where to begin. She traced the pattern in the sofa cushion with her fingernail, and said, "This entire month with you has been wonderful, Mitch. You've been so self-assured, so composed ever since I met you. Even being thrust into the role of Joey's father didn't change that."

"He's my son."

"I know, and you love him and I admire you for it."

"Does that bother you?"

Her gaze met his across the span of one sofa cushion. "No, I meant it when I said I admired you for the way you've taken Joey into your home, into your heart. It's just that I haven't thought about having kids in years. I may never be ready for motherhood. I've never met anyone like you before, and I can't let you get hurt."

"Raine." His voice was deep, his tone completely serious. "First of all, I haven't asked you to bear our children, and secondly, whether or not I end up hurt isn't your responsibility." He reached for her hand. Spreading her fingers, he slipped them in between each of his.

"But—"

"And thirdly, *easygoing people can't take responsibility for everyone else.* No one can."

"I don't want to see you get hurt."

"And I don't want to see you get hurt." Leaning toward her, he grazed her mouth with his lips.

"But what about Joey?" she asked.

He slowly lowered her with him until her back rested on the carpet. "I've thought about that, wondered if he might become too attached to you. But honestly, Raine, I don't see how knowing you could ever hurt him. You are a very special woman."

"Mitch, what am I going to do with you?"

Propping himself on his elbows, he leaned over her and began to whisper a few suggestions. As her eyes stared into his, his voice dipped to guttural tones. With the third suggestion, Raine began to laugh. By the time he'd murmured number seven, the laughter had seeped out of her.

She never dreamed anyone's voice could warm her so thoroughly. Her desire for Mitch overrode her worries, blocked her responsibilities from her mind. She was fully aware of the heat radiating from his body, was fully aware of every firm, hard inch of him pressed so tightly to her. She was fully aware of his passion, of his need. And she was becoming increasingly aware of her own needs.

Mitch kissed her again. Slowly. Thoroughly. He raised his face from hers, then immediately rolled to his side. Raine sat up, wondering what he was waiting for. He had to know she wanted him, so why was he holding himself back?

"I'm going to have to add another category to describe dentists," she declared.

He seemed to be having a difficult time bringing his breathing under control. She watched his chest expand with the effort, and saw him rake his fingers through his hair. She waited for him to look at her. When he finally did, she cast him a quick wink and said, "The third category of dentists are virile, charming to a fault, incredibly innovative and as stubborn as mules."

His deep chuckle rumbled in his chest. Another rumble, in the vicinity of his stomach, soon followed. With a decadent look, he said, "Don't move. I'll start the steaks, and be right back."

After he'd left the room, Raine looked around her. His place was still as neat as could be. The only articles out of order were two throw pillows, and one of Raine's shoes. She slipped it on her foot, then searched the floor for the other one.

She peeked around the doorway at Mitch, who was on the deck, seasoning steaks on the grill. He was still barefoot, although he had buttoned his shirt.

Maybe she could just relax and enjoy what they shared. Maybe he really did want exactly what she did—to live for today. He didn't seem concerned that Joey would become too attached to her, had decided it wasn't a problem.

Going down on her hands and knees, she felt beneath the sofa for her shoe. She didn't believe how close she'd come to making love on the floor. It was so unlike her. But, she realized, thanks to Mitch, she was discovering a lot of new experiences. She could just imagine his reaction if she said something about it to him. "Rule number three hundred and seventeen," he'd say. "Easygoing people react to spontaneous situations in spontaneous ways."

Reaching her hand farther under the sofa, she came in contact with one of Tanner's rubber balls, a magazine, an empty potato chip wrapper and one of Joey's toy trucks. Evidently, Eva hadn't cleaned under here.

"Aha!" she declared, when she finally pulled her shoe from the mess beneath his sofa. And then she noticed that a photograph had fluttered out with her shoe. A photograph of a woman—a gorgeous woman.

Chapter Nine

"How do you like your steak?" Mitch called from the doorway.

"Medium," Raine answered, still mesmerized by the beautiful woman's photograph. Turning it over, she slid her foot into her shoe and carried the picture out to the deck. "What's this?" she asked, holding the photo toward him.

"A picture."

"No kidding. Who is she?"

"I have no idea. Her photograph arrived in the mail on Saturday while I was with you, taking a balloon ride through the wild blue yonder. You do remember that ride, don't you?"

"Vaguely," she teased. "Who'd send you a picture of a beautiful woman?"

"Who do you think?"

"Kyle," they declared in unison.

"Or maybe Taylor," Mitch added.

"But why?"

The steaks sizzled on the grill. Tanner dozed on a layer of dry leaves in the corner and Mitch leaned against the deck's railing, his feet spread a comfortable distance apart, his arms folded at his chest. He slid his hands to her waist and pulled her closer, until her hips rested at the juncture of his thighs.

"It goes back a long way. It all started when we were barely in our teens. Taylor was thirteen and had a crush on an older girl, so Kyle and I bet him he'd never have the courage to ask her out. He won that bet and demanded something for his trouble. We gave him one of our dad's old bowling trophies."

"What a prize!"

"We never thought he'd accept that old trophy as payment, but he loved it. Since then, it's been passed back and forth dozens of times."

"What does that have to do with this photograph?"

Mitch's fingers found their way to the soft skin at Raine's waist where he traced half circles on her flesh. Goose bumps started where he touched, then climbed outward to her limbs.

"I'm getting to that."

"That's not all your getting to."

"Do you mind?" His voice dipped lower as he settled her more comfortably against him.

She stared into his eyes. How could she possibly mind, when he was making her feel so happy? "Um, Mitch, I think you're burning our steaks."

Releasing her, he moved back to the grill. He turned the gas off, then flipped the steaks onto the plate. "Dinner is served."

Seated at Mitch's small dining-room table a few minutes later, Raine asked Mitch to continue his bowling trophy story.

"Okay, you asked for it. After Taylor won the trophy that first time, there were more bets, and that old bowling trophy made the rounds between the three of us. I once held it for dating twins, simultaneously, in the eleventh grade." He raised his eyebrows.

"Fiend."

"When you've got it, you've got it. Taylor dated one of the Dallas Cowboy cheerleaders. Kyle took it away from him when he dated an astronaut a couple years ago."

Raine shook her head and waited for him to continue.

"We'd all forgotten about those bets until a couple months ago when the three of us went to our cousin's wedding. Stag. As the evening wore on, and believe me it was wearing, every aunt, uncle and cousin asked us the same thing. *'Still single, boys?'* Then they proceeded to advise us on the intricacies of snagging a good woman.

"By the end of the night, we were all fed up. Since they're both completely juvenile when it comes to that trophy, Kyle challenged Taylor and I to a bet. The brother who shows up with a fiancée or wife at our parent's wedding anniversary party next month will win *it*. Permanently."

"Mitch, that's perfect!"

"What's perfect?"

"You can win that trophy back from Kyle. I'll go with you to your party. Kyle and Taylor don't know this is just a...just a..."

"Just a what, Raine?"

Mitch's grim expression made her hesitate. Jerking his chair out, he stood. Without looking at her, he stacked her plate on top of his.

As he strode to the counter, she tried again. "Come on, you're the one who's always telling me easygoing people go with the flow."

"No!" The plates clattered to the bottom of the sink with the force of that one word.

"Why not?" Raine felt a dull ache of foreboding. Her words hung in the air between them for several seconds.

Mitch slid his hand into his pocket. The material began to move as he rattled his loose change. After a moment, he pulled it out again, flexing his fingers. As if he'd given his answer much consideration, he placed both hands on his hips, squared his jaw and finally met her gaze. "If you go with me, it has to be for real. No jokes. No tricks."

"But, Mitch, I thought you understood. That's what I was trying to tell you before dinner. This isn't a permanent relationship."

"I understand. You were honest with me. Now I'm being honest with you."

She pushed her hair from her eyes, her hope that theirs could remain a casual interlude dashed by his words. Even though he'd placed no demands on her, she was beginning to feel caged in. "Where does that leave us?"

"Exactly where we were before we had this conversation. In limbo. And I'm trying to live with that."

He hadn't said the word *love*, but it glittered from his eyes. Raine wondered how long it had been there. She was normally so observant. Why hadn't she seen? Guilt dropped like a rock to the pit of her stomach. "But you deserve more. I've never known anyone like you. What will you get from this relationship?"

"The same things you're getting. A lot of fun. A wonderful adventure." Mitch strode toward her. "Come on, Raine, lighten up. Easygoing people don't worry so much."

"Then maybe I was never meant to be an easygoing person."

"Raine, don't look so worried. I'm not Clay or Holly or your neighbor's cats or your co-workers. You're not responsible for me. I can take care of myself."

"But—"

His telephone rang, interrupting any further argument. Mitch grabbed it up like an opportunity. He'd never been so relieved to hear Taylor's voice. His younger brother didn't know it, but he'd probably just bought Mitch more time. "Hold on, Taylor," he said before turning back to Raine.

"Taylor and I have to go over some of the details for our parents' party."

"That's exactly the kind of job Clarissa just hired me to do. I can help you," she promised.

"I think we've got it covered." He propelled her toward the door where he kissed her soundly on the mouth. "Congratulations on your new job. We never got around to talking about that, did we? I want to hear all about it tomorrow." He brushed his lips over hers once more, practically pushing her through the door.

Gripping the phone, he took a gulp of air before he said, "Yeah, I'm still here, Taylor, what's happening?" It took several minutes before his heart rate had returned to normal.

He'd breathed a sigh of relief when she'd accepted his words before dinner, when he'd told her she wasn't responsible for him. And the way she'd responded to him, right in the middle of the living-room floor, had convinced him she'd come to want more. It was becoming increasingly difficult to resist her, but until she realized he wasn't one of her responsibilities, he had to.

She'd come here tonight to talk about her concern that Joey might be getting too attached to her. He'd never known another woman like her, had never known anyone who cared so deeply for others.

But she still wasn't free. He remembered the day he'd seen her in the park, the day she'd been flying her kite. Raine equated freedom with the sky. But she wasn't any more free than that kite had been. Her strings bound her to earth just as surely as the kite's. She just didn't know it.

"Yeah, Taylor, I'm listening." he said again, when his brother practically yelled across the phone lines.

He'd entered into this *adventure* because he was attracted to Raine. Who wouldn't be? He'd loved the thrill of the chase, the challenge. But he'd known, almost from the beginning, there was more involved than a challenge. He'd fallen in love. He wanted Raine, forever. And she wanted a fling. How had this whole thing backfired?

"Okay," he said into the phone. "I'll call the caterer, you call the florist. Kyle had better have taken care of the invitations or it'll be one small party. I don't know about you but I'll be glad when it's over."

Mitch hung up, noticing the photograph he'd received anonymously through the mail. Closing his long fingers over the picture, he squeezed until the woman's face became contorted into a crumpled ball. The action brought him little satisfaction. He pretended to execute two fancy dribbles on the carpet before throwing the photograph toward the wastebasket across the room.

Casting a questioning look to his master, Tanner padded to the corner and retrieved the ball of paper from the floor nearby. When Mitch didn't make any move to stop him, he proceeded to rip the photo to shreds.

With an unsettling sense of foreboding, Mitch watched his pet gnaw on the paper, and had a feeling that's exactly where his future with Raine was headed. To the dogs.

"To the dogs," Eva declared to Mitch on her last evening in Pennsylvania. She flipped off the late news and sputtered, "This country is going to the dogs." She reached for her herb tea and continued. "I feel sorry for the little ones today. This country's really going to be a mess by the time they're grown."

Mitch knew he didn't have to respond. He'd actually gotten used to Eva's opinions, although he rarely agreed with them.

"It's Raine, isn't it?"

"What?" he asked absently.

"The reason you're so quiet." Mitch started to protest, and she effectively interrupted him. "I know I have no right to tell you what to do, and God only knows how much I appreciate what you've done for me this week, what with inviting me, a virtual stranger to stay with you and all, not to mention what you've done for Joey. I see the way you look at Raine. I may need trifocals, but I'm not blind. I said to myself, Eva, I said, why do you suppose Mitch's folks have never heard of a woman both Mitch and Joey are obviously in love with?''

"You mentioned Raine to my parents?''

"Discreetly, mind you.''

Mitch just bet.

"When I first saw Joey have one of his temper tantrums, it reminded me of Elizabeth. She was a stubborn child, but kind, too." Eva took an embroidered handkerchief from her sleeve and dabbed at her eyes. "And smart... my, she was smart. She wanted to have a child, so she set off to find a suitable man. Now, I'm not condoning what she did. I'm just saying she chose well. Not only a smart and handsome man, but a caring one, too."

Now that Mitch thought about it, Elizabeth hadn't filled her own glass nearly as often as she'd filled his. At the time, he hadn't noticed. He should have harbored a grudge or been appalled that Elizabeth's seduction of him had been premeditated. Out of a thousand dentists at that convention, she'd chosen him to father her child. For some reason, Mitch couldn't even work up an ounce of old-fashioned macho conceit.

He took a sip of his chamomile tea and grimaced at the horrid flavor. Eva swore it would help him sleep, and Mitch figured it was worth a shot. He sure hadn't been sleeping well these past several nights without it.

"Now, I won't lie and say it didn't bother me the first time I saw Joey in Raine's arms, but after talking to her, I realized she was a fine woman, and what with my Elizabeth gone, I figured Raine would be good to Joey. At first, I wondered what was holding you back, why you didn't snap a ring on her finger and have yourselves a couple more kids. But *you* aren't what's holding you back, are you, Mitch?''

Mitch wanted to banish the thoughts her words evoked. All along he'd been confident that Raine would grow to love him. He didn't know how much longer he'd be able to deny the evidence. He didn't know how much longer he'd be able to settle for an honest affair.

"I'm not saying she doesn't have her reasons, but I hope she comes around. My arthritis can't take these wet eastern winters, so I won't be staying around to see for myself. You just let me know if there's anything I can do to help.''

Raine ran her hand over the surface of the old trunk Mitch had helped her sand weeks ago. Now, completely smooth and stained a deep walnut, it stood at the foot of her bed, a constant reminder of the time they'd spent together.

The antique mantel clock chimed the hour from downstairs. Mitch was late as usual. She hadn't expected him to be the type of man who enjoyed shopping, but he'd said he wanted to tag along when she went looking for clothes to wear for her new job.

Mitch had been full of surprises since the day she met him. He made her laugh, made her feel as if her life was an incredible adventure. He was fun and alluring and charming. He took life as it came, plain and simple. Why couldn't she be like that? She wanted to throw caution to the wind, to embrace life. But something always held her back.

Eva had returned to Arizona, and Mitch was as fun-loving as he'd always been. But their relationship had changed. Raine *felt* different. There was only one word to describe her new emotion—guilty. She couldn't seem to rid herself of the feeling that she was short-changing Mitch.

He'd said he and his brothers weren't so completely unorganized they couldn't plan their parents' anniversary party and hadn't given in to her pleas to let her help, to relieve at least a small portion of her guilt. He was adamant about it, and she realized he wasn't quite as cool and composed as she'd thought. She was beginning to discover a stubborn streak in Mitch, one a mile wide.

Hugging her arms to her body, she tread down the steps and perched on the sofa, her foot instantly beginning to jiggle, her mind a tangle of confusion. Worry knotted her stomach and she knew she couldn't go on this way. Mitch really did understand about her dream. But he had dreams, too, and she couldn't let him settle for anything less. If she could just get him to tell her what his dreams were.

Before the doorbell's chime ended, Raine had jumped to her feet. She grabbed her purse and jacket and ran down the last flight of stairs. One way or another, she'd find out what he really wanted, what he dreamed of. No matter what he said about easygoing people not being responsible for other people's feelings, she couldn't risk hurting him.

Hours later, she and Mitch both carried several shopping bags. She now had enough dresses and suits and blouses to begin her new job. Mitch had given his opinion on every one. It hadn't taken her long to discover he preferred dresses to slacks. And the shorter and tighter the better.

"Mitch!" she'd whispered. "I need clothes to wear to work at weddings, not stag parties."

"I'm only giving you my opinions. If you'd rather buy old-lady clothes..."

She couldn't remember ever having more fun shopping. He'd kept the conversation and the atmosphere light. Each time she'd tried to talk about what he wanted, he steered the discussion in another direction. Hadn't she always known he was smooth?

On their way out of the mall, Mitch pulled her into a novelty shop. In the spirit of good, old-fashioned fun, they flipped through license plates and posters. Holding up a *Philadelphia, the land of brotherly love* bumper sticker, Raine said, "You should buy one for Taylor and Kyle."

He looked up from the license plates he'd been studying and shook his head. Something in his eyes drew her gaze to the license plate in his hand. *I Love My Dentist*. She looked into his face, and they both looked away. Neither of them said a word, but Raine had glimpsed the yearning in his eyes.

In the parking lot outside, the sky had turned dark and the wind blew cold. Raine shivered beneath her jacket. After Mitch unlocked her door, she slid inside and waited. He climbed in beside her and rubbed his hands together.

She wasn't falling for his casual facade, not this time. "Mitch, if you could have anything, anything in the world, what would it be?"

"What kind of a question is that?"

"I want to know."

"Why?"

Raine looked directly into his eyes. "Because I *need* to know. What do you really want?"

Trying to make light of the situation, he said, "Well, it wouldn't be Eva's tea, that's for sure."

"Seriously, Mitch. What do you want?"

It took him several seconds to answer. "If I could have anything I wanted, anything in the world, I'd have you."

Tears gathered in her eyes. "What else?"

"What do you mean what else?"

"What else do you want?"

"Raine." He ran his hand through his hair. She saw the tension in his jaw, the worry in his eyes.

"What else, Mitch?"

"You aren't going to stop until I answer, are you?"

She shook her head.

He took a deep breath. "I'd like to live with you, in a house with lots of stairs, in the country, where Joey and Tanner can play."

She didn't answer. She couldn't. The light from the parking lot cast a pale glow across Mitch's face, bleaching out all colors but black, white and silver. He was gazing outside, his mouth set in a straight line.

"I don't know what to say," she whispered.

"There isn't anything to say." Without looking at her, Mitch started his car, then slowly backed from the parking space.

He wants a family. Raine felt hollow. She'd been afraid of what he might say, but had asked because she didn't want to hurt him. She knew it was too late for that now.

"Raine, don't look so sad. Who knows what the future holds? For now, let's enjoy what we have."

She squeezed his large hand, as much to reassure herself as to reassure him, and wished she hadn't asked him what he needed. Now that she knew, what could she do? She'd never lived for the moment. She didn't know if she could do it now.

He pulled up in front of her house and turned her face to his. He lowered his head, brushing his lips across hers. She didn't close her eyes and neither did he. When the kiss ended, she gathered up her shopping bags, and slid from the car. She fit her key in the lock, and didn't turn at the sound of his tires squealing away from the curb.

"I've had the most exhausting day! If you think I never sit still, you should see Clarissa. The phones never stopped ringing. Holly called when I got home tonight. Do you know what I said when I answered?"

When Mitch shook his head, she rushed on. "*Weddings, Parties & More.* I've been there one week and I've ordered flowers from a florist who speaks Hungarian, argued with a shifty bookkeeper, calmed an overwrought bride-to-be and warded off the advances of a feisty father-of-the-bride."

"And you loved every minute of it." The warmth of his smile shone from his eyes, echoed in his voice. Raine slowed her steps along the winding park trail, then completely stopped. His look was gentle, and she felt confused by her conflicting emotions.

Joey ran ahead and Mitch stopped to pick up a fallen stick, whistled for Tanner, and threw it out in the other direction. She'd brought up the subject of his parents' anniversary party several times. Each time, he'd stubbornly refused her offer to help. The subject hadn't come up again. But it was there between them.

Planning parties was what she now did for a living, yet Mitch wouldn't let her help him plan this one. Raine knew why. It was because she'd defined their relationship: no strings, no commitments, no responsibilities.

Leaves whirling on the autumn breeze brought her mind back to the present. Tanner's feet crunched over the dry leaves and, with his tail wagging and his ears flying, he dropped the twig at her feet, looking from Raine to his master.

She bent to retrieve the stick. Mitch did the same. When they grasped it at opposite ends, her gaze was drawn to his hand. With a gasp, Raine took his hand in hers, staring at the ugly welt on his finger. Shards of light spun in her head. She blinked away the feeling of weakness and whispered, "What happened?"

"The next time a five-year-old tells me I can't look in her mouth, I'm going to listen."

She smoothed her fingertips over the mark and, raising his hand to her mouth, gently kissed the tip of his finger. Mitch made a sound deep in his throat. His arms came around her, pulling her hard against him. His head swooped down, capturing her mouth, capturing her breath, capturing a piece of her heart.

Raine had known there was something special about Mitch from the beginning. She'd thought long and hard about him, about his needs. She knew a part of her loved him. She also knew she couldn't give him the rest of her heart. She could give him everything else, but not that. A hot ache grew in her throat because he deserved more.

She felt her time with Mitch was drawing to an end. With heartfelt desperation, she opened her mouth under his, and felt a deep sigh pass from her mouth to his.

They'd been together often these past two weeks. Each time Raine had felt a growing sense of urgency, as if something wonderful was ending. Now, they drew apart bit by bit, first their mouths parted, then their faces lifted, finally their bodies straightened.

Raine opened her eyes and she fought a bit of dizziness. She slid her arm around Mitch's back and he fit his hand to her waist. They began to stroll along the trail, the leaves crunching beneath their feet, Joey happily bouncing amidst the foliage beside them.

"I remember the first time I saw you in this park. I was flying my kite," Raine murmured. That had been the beginning of September. The leaves had been green then. Now, only the most stubborn leaves clung to otherwise bare branches. "Two days until Halloween," she said softly.

"Halloween is good for business." At her questioning expression, he added, "All those treats the kids eat are terrible for their teeth."

His comment made her smile. He always made her smile.

The leaves scattered when she kicked through them, and it was suddenly all she could do to force her leg muscles to support her. "It's been a wonderful autumn." She turned her head to gaze up at him. His eyes were the color of blue smoke. His mouth, the mouth she'd kissed a hundred times, was full. And unsmiling.

He was holding a part of himself back. He wasn't pushing her for a commitment, and the strain showed in his eyes. She wished she could give him what he wanted, what he deserved. For ten years she'd given everything she had. To Holly and Clay and nearly everyone she knew. Now she was afraid, afraid she'd wake up one morning with nothing left to give.

"You hungry?" Mitch asked.

She rested her head on his shoulder. "I'd better just go home. I think I'm coming down with something. I'll call you, okay?"

Tanner lifted his head as Mitch stomped by. Nine o'clock on a Saturday morning and Mitch felt no closer to a solution than he'd been five hours ago. He'd picked up Joey from the babysitter and they'd driven into Philadelphia after work last night to go over the final details of his parents' anniversary party with Taylor and Kyle. No wonder Clarissa's business was growing so rapidly. People were willing to pay, and pay dearly, just to have someone else see to all the details for these crazy parties.

He'd decided to drive back home late last night, just on the off chance that Raine might have called. But there was no message on his answering machine. He hadn't heard from her since they'd walked in the park earlier in the week. Not one word.

Pressure was building inside him, in his chest, in his gut—and lower. He paced from the television where Joey was watching cartoons and building a tower out of blocks, to his bedroom, then back out again. Memories of Raine assailed him. Memories of her laughter, and warm brown eyes, of her jiggling foot and her full-power kisses.

There had been times she'd nearly come apart in his arms. Those instances he could almost believe she loved him. Then, she'd suddenly pull back, as if she were fighting against him for her freedom. She had so many reasons to feel the way she felt. He was trying to understand them all. And he didn't know what to do about any of them.

One thing upset him, more than everything else combined. When he'd first met her, she was struggling with her newfound independence. But she'd been happy. She wasn't happy anymore.

She'd taken to jiggling her foot again. She was restless. Each time he looked into her eyes, he saw something that disturbed him. Her dark brown eyes were flecked with worry, etched with confusion and filled with guilt. Why did she feel guilty? Because she didn't love him?

She hadn't wanted to spend any more time with him after their walk in the park, not even to get something to eat. She'd said she was coming down with something. What was coming was *the end*. He'd known it for two weeks. He'd tried to keep it light, to keep it fun, but she'd seen through him like a picture window.

He'd give anything to hear her laughter, to see her eyes crinkle with humor, to see that blasted foot of hers stop jiggling. To have her call.

No matter how much he paced, no matter how often he stared at the phone, it didn't ring. Before the waiting made him crazier, he grabbed the phone and called Jennifer Tornelli, the reliable teenager from down the street. When she arrived to watch Joey, Mitch flicked his jacket from the back of a chair and searched for his keys. He'd waited long enough. It was time to set this bird free.

Minutes later, Clay looked up from beneath the hood of Raine's little car. Of course she had time for her brother, yet she hadn't taken one minute to call him. Mitch's temper began a slow simmer. Without saying a word to Clay, he took the back steps two at a time.

The combined aromas of several heady spices bombarded his nostrils the instant he opened the door. Raine had taken the time to cook, but she hadn't taken the time to call him. His simmering temper began to boil.

Lengthening his stride, he marched past the laundry room where the washer swished and the dryer hummed. Raine was obviously keeping herself busy, very busy. From the corner of his eye, he caught a glimpse of movement near the floor in the kitchen. Mitch watched as an errant strand of blond hair was tucked behind an ear. Long blond hair.

"Holly."

"Shh!" Raine's sister shrieked, jumping to her feet. "Good grief, Mitch. Are you trying to scare me to death? Quiet. Rainie's sleeping."

"Sleeping? At this hour?"

"She's sick. She's had a horrible case of the flu. Didn't she tell you?"

Mitch shook his head. Terrible regrets assailed him. He'd thought the worst. She'd needed him and he'd thought the worst. No wonder she hadn't called. She was sick. She hadn't wanted to eat because she really *was* coming down with something. No wonder she hadn't called.

She should have called, dammit.

Holly, obviously in a chatting mood, went back to her task of washing Raine's floor. "Clay came here last night. Guess he needed to have a button sewn on, or something..."

Mitch slid his hand into his pocket. Clay was twenty-one years old. He was old enough to vote. You'd think he was old enough to sew on one tiny button.

"But when he saw how sick Rainie was, he canceled his date and called me."

"It was good of you and Clay to help," Mitch said absently.

"Where else would we be? We're family. You know Rainie. She'd never *ask* for help."

He knew Raine, all right. He knew why she didn't ask for help. That was the trouble with those totally independent, freedom-seeking people.

He left Holly to the kitchen floor and began to wander around the first level of Raine's home, realizing he couldn't disturb her rest to talk this problem out. No matter where he turned, he felt in the way. Raine and Holly and Clay were a family unit. He was just a fling, an adventure.

He ambled back out the same way he'd come. His hand, hidden from sight, jingled the loose change in his pocket. He'd known Raine was the woman he wanted to spend the rest of his life with. Sure, he'd known she wanted freedom, but he'd been confident it was only a matter of time before she realized what she really wanted was him. He'd thought her quest for adventure and fun was less important than his quest for her.

Her quest for freedom wasn't frivolous. It wasn't something she simply wanted. Understanding finally dawned. Raine *needed* her freedom, needed it even more than she needed his love.

Mitch watched Clay wipe his hands on a cloth, then close the hood. "Are you good with cars?" Mitch asked.

Clay looked him over, as if he were sizing him up. With a cockiness that came with youth, he answered, "I like to think I am. Are you?"

"No. Toothaches and basketballs are more or less my specialties."

Mitch had the distinct feeling Clay was memorizing not only everything he said, but the *way* he said it, too. Oh, no, he thought, not another totally observant McAlister.

"Basketballs, huh? Feel up to a game with me?"

Mitch read the challenge in Clay's look. He'd never felt more like pulverizing someone in an honest game of one-on-one in his life. "You're on." Anything was better than wandering around in a house where he didn't belong.

"Come on. Cloudie's neighbor a couple of houses down has a hoop."

An hour later, Mitch was bent over, hands on knees, trying to catch his breath. Two cats had witnessed the entire game from the sill of a tall window. Clay, the young punk, didn't even look winded. Mitch's narrow victory was his only consolation.

Clay spun the ball on his finger. "So, you're in love with my sister."

It hadn't been a question, but a statement. Mitch straightened and took another deep breath, looking at Raine's brother, eye to eye. Clay suddenly seemed older, more like a solicitous father than a spoiled little brother.

"So, are you movin' in?"

Mitch thought about telling Clay it was none of his business, but something in the younger man's look halted his words. For the first time in weeks, Mitch felt himself begin to relax. In that instant, he faced something he'd been hiding from for a long time. He'd met the right woman, and it was time to do the right thing.

He settled his hands on his hips and, with conviction steadying his voice, he said, "No, Clay. I'm not moving in. I knew the day I met Raine that she wanted to be independent. Now I know it isn't only what she wants. It's what she needs."

Clay looked away. From the way he began dribbling the basketball, it was obvious he was trying to choose his words carefully. "It wasn't easy for Raine when our parents died. I mean, she was only Holly's age, and she had to take care of us."

"Now you and Holly are taking care of her."

That about summed it up. Holly and Clay didn't need Raine to take care of them anymore. She was free of the responsibility of her brother and sister. Free of a job she had never liked. Free to take chances, to experience adventure. There was only one other thing she needed to be free of.

"Think fast!"

Mitch caught the ball out of self-defense.

"I'm sorry things aren't working out, man."

"Yeah, me, too." They walked back to Raine's tiny yard where Mitch helped Clay wash her car. Then, leaving Clay behind to wax it, he wandered back inside. He loved her, and because he did, he was going to let her go.

Chapter Ten

Raine looked up the moment Mitch walked through her back door. She was sitting at her tiny kitchen table, and the sight of Mitch made her want to cry.

Holly suddenly appeared, ladling soup into another bowl. "Doesn't Rainie look like a ghost?"

"She looks beautiful."

Tears swam in Raine's eyes. She knew exactly how she looked. Pale, weak and horrid.

Holly discreetly disappeared, and Mitch sat down across from Raine. Pushing the soup away, he said, "Those two have really come through for you this time. You've done a wonderful job of raising them. They're grown-up now."

She bit her lip, and wavered a smile his way.

"I wish we could go on the way we've been, but I can't, Raine, and neither can you. We're both turning into nervous wrecks. And you're right, I have Joey to think about, too."

She reached her hand across the table, covering his bony knuckles. "Of course you do. He's one lucky little boy, you know that?"

"You told me the first time we met that you were on the brink of a whole new life. You told me you wanted to be free, wanted to have fun, wanted your life to be an adventure. You didn't just want those things. You *needed* them. You still do."

He smiled at her, and her heart nearly turned over. "I'm sorry, Mitch."

"I'm sorry things didn't work out the way I wanted, but I'm not sorry I met you," he whispered. Leaning toward her, he brushed his lips across hers, one last time. "Don't forget, Raine. If you ever need me, call. *Mitchell W. Harris* at your service."

A tear dropped from her eye and trailed down her face. Mitch was letting her go, physically, and emotionally. She could feel it in his kiss, see it in his eyes. He was setting her free, in a way no one ever had before.

He didn't smile, and neither did she. He gave her hand a squeeze. And then he was gone.

The noise of the small plane's engine made talking nearly impossible. Raine gave her flight instructor a thumbs-up sign, and closed the door, closing out the cold November wind.

She swallowed. Hard. An unfamiliar sound seeped into her brain. After a moment, she realized it was the sound of her heart pounding in her chest. It felt as if wild horses were stampeding inside her rib cage. Raine struggled to take in a deep breath as she checked gauges, flipped switches. This sudden case of nerves surprised her. She'd gone over and over this entire procedure. She knew exactly what to do, yet she couldn't shake the feeling that something wasn't quite right. Something was missing.

She'd wanted to fly all her life. Instead of feeling a wonderful sense of anticipation because she was about to experience her life's dream, she felt sad. Raine was certain of only one thing. Before she could go on with the rest of her life, she *had* to make this solo flight.

She gulped in several steadying breaths, and flipped another switch. Grasping the control, she began her taxi down the runway. In her heart she knew she was ready. It was her time to soar.

She held the control with just the right amount of pressure, increasing the plane's speed. At exactly the right moment, she pushed up on the control, and she was airborne. Her rapid climb sucked the oxygen out of her lungs. Her stomach must have stayed on the ground. It certainly wasn't where it was supposed to be.

She was soaring into a blue so clear, she felt it would never end. With her eyes wide open she looked all around her and experienced the thrill of flying. A change flowed through her and her body nearly vibrated with a new sense of peace.

Exactly as she'd been taught, Raine watched the dials and instruments, turning and swooping and soaring beneath the clouds. The view was spectacular, but it wasn't the reason she felt a smile pull at her lips.

"Oh, Mitch," she whispered. Her thoughts became so silent, it was as if a hush had fallen over the world. She'd heard of people's entire lives flashing before their eyes. Raine suddenly saw her entire relationship with Mitch flash before hers. She saw his slow, steady smile, the one that sent her stomach into a three-hundred-sixty-degree spin. She remembered the texture of his hair, the way it curled after a shower. She remembered more than his physical characteristics. She felt as if she were remembering Mitch from the inside out.

She pictured him as he'd walked away. It had taken all her strength to keep from calling him back. She couldn't do that to him, couldn't offer him less than he deserved. Guilt had assailed her as she'd watched him walk down the back steps, watched as he waved to Clay and as he drove down the back alley. The memory turned her heart upside down, made her temples throb, her chest ache. As she struggled to regain her composure, everything about Mitch became crystal-clear, as clear as the air through which she now flew.

She took one hand off the control, and spread it over her heart. Her chest had felt like a cool, dark cave, her heart a cold slab of loneliness. Something had been gnawing at her insides all week. It had to do with Mitch and how much she missed him. It had to do with dreams, and desires.

She looked at the barren fields to the west, at the hills dotted with rocks and trees to the north. She looked above her at the clouds. Then she looked down at the landing area, where flags and lines marked the runway. There was no safety net.

So many thoughts chased through her mind, thoughts about life, more specifically, those events in a person's life that shaped their future. Elizabeth Russell had felt her biological clock ticking, and had set out to have a child, a child she'd always dreamed she'd have. Elizabeth's dream had altered her life, and Mitch's. That alteration was named Joey.

Raine's parents had died ten years ago, altering the course *her* life would take. Then, a few months ago, another accident, this one coming close to taking *her* life, had sent Raine into a tailspin, forcing her to take another look at her own dreams.

She examined her dreams now. She'd thought her freedom would keep her safe from hurt. She now realized life had no safety net, no guarantee for happiness. She'd let Mitch walk away because she thought she needed her freedom. She now realized freedom was only an illusion.

Mitch would probably spout some silly rule. *Easygoing people soar on a wing and a prayer.*

How many times had her thoughts turned to Mitch this past week? Fifty? A hundred? A million times? She wished he and Joey were watching, waiting for her down below. She wished she could share this great adventure with them.

As she banked the plane and began her gradual descent, realization dawned, clear and potent. She loved Mitch. She'd thought he'd tie her down. Instead, he'd set her free.

She loved him. Raine suddenly understood why her heart had felt so cold. She'd let the most important person in her life walk away. What good was freedom if she had no one to share it with? What good was love if she had no one to give it to?

The plane wobbled a little, and Raine grasped the control with both hands, her heart in her throat. The plane evened off, and she did exactly as she'd been taught, exactly as she'd done when her instructor had been sitting in the seat beside her. She was coming in a little faster than she had before, but the wheels touched down, and she kept the control steady, nice and steady.

Moments later, the plane was taxiing down the runway, and her fellow classmates, along with their instructor, let out loud whoops, throwing their hats, and anything else they could find, into the air.

She'd done it. She'd flown through the wild blue yonder.

But her pleasure was short-lived, her joy obscured. Mitch hadn't witnessed her victory. She'd felt guilty because she couldn't give him what he wanted. Her, a family, a lifetime commitment. Because she'd already raised Holly and Clay, having the responsibility of a lasting relationship had scared her half to death. But Clay and Holly were her brother and sister, not her children. She'd raised them all alone. That complete aloneness had been her cage.

The wind whipped her hair away from her face as she opened the door. Everyone was suddenly there, helping her down, hugging her, clapping her on the back. They didn't seem to notice that her cheers were only halfhearted.

She'd wanted to fly all her life. And although she'd loved it, it wasn't really the experience to end all experiences. She thought her dream was to be carefree, to fly. Now, she realized that sharing her life with Mitch could have been a wonderful adventure. The adventure of a lifetime. Their unity would have been her freedom.

She could have met someone who made demands, who insisted his needs were greater than hers, who wouldn't have wanted her to be independent. Instead, she'd met Mitch. Through her relationship with him, she'd become aware of a strong passion within her, and had come to recognize her own needs.

Raine shivered, not so much from the wind but from the vivid recollection of Mitch's smile and touch, of the love shining in his eyes. She wished she could fly to him right now.

She said goodbye to her friends, and hurried to her car, turning the key with shaking fingers. Worry stabbed at her heart, clenched tight in her stomach. She had to find a way to convince Mitch she loved him. After all the times she'd insisted she *needed* her freedom, she was afraid it wasn't going to be easy to convince him she'd been wrong.

Taylor and Kyle were arguing about the proper way to set up folding chairs in the living room when the doorbell rang. With a shake of his head at his brothers' adolescent behavior, Mitch checked on Joey, then strode to the front hall. A short, bald man who seemed to be hiding behind a large floral centerpiece was leaning on the blasted doorbell. The man bustled past him in a huff. "Where do you want this?"

"Taylor!" Mitch shouted, "you're in charge of flowers. Where do you want this arrangement?"

Taylor jogged into the front hallway where he ran his hand through his hair. "Search me. I guess you could put it on the dining-room table for now."

The front doorbell rang again. An instant later, the telephone rang, followed immediately by a loud knock, this time on the back door. The three brothers looked at one another.

"Remind me never to have a fortieth wedding anniversary party," Kyle grumbled.

"That shouldn't be a problem since you couldn't even get a *date* for this afternoon," Taylor taunted.

"Look who's talking," Kyle returned.

"Guys," Mitch rumbled. "I'll get the phone, you two get the doors and try not to trip over Joey in the process." He grabbed the telephone off the wall. "Hello," he snapped into the mouthpiece and wondered if this day would ever end.

He held the receiver away from his ear as a shrill voice reprimanded him. Aunt Millie was all he needed. "Sorry, Aunt Millie. I'm afraid tensions are a little high around here this morning." He was thirty-five years old, yet one word from Millie Harris and he felt eight all over again.

Mitch barely listened to Millie's tirade. The truth was, he'd been in a foul mood all week. His disposition wasn't likely to improve as the day wore on. The florist huffed past him, then nearly collided with the caterers who in turn almost upset the woman from the bakery who was delivering the cake. The level of chaos only increased from that point.

The brother's parents, Ed and Mary Harris breezed into the room, their faces cheerful, their smiles sunny even if it was beginning to drizzle outside. Mary looked radiant as she gazed from her husband to her grown sons.

Mitch watched his father's eyes soften as his gaze settled on his wife of forty years. Mitch recognized that look. It was the way he'd looked at Raine. He slid his hand into his pocket, his fingers automatically searching for something to rattle. Instead of keys or loose change, they smoothed over a folded sheet of paper.

He'd grabbed the mail on his way out the door yesterday. He'd absently opened the first envelope, and wished he hadn't. It was an itemized billing for his charge card, and one item in particular had caught his attention. Lingerie. From Leslie Anne's Boutique, where he'd purchased Raine's birthday gift.

The memories that had overtaken him then overtook him now. Memories of the look in Raine's eyes when he'd given her that teddy, memories of the day they'd taken the balloon ride along the edge of the Pocono Mountains. He'd stuffed the bill in his pocket, along with his thoughts.

Mary Harris bent to pick Joey up, exclaiming over his plaid knickers and red suspenders. Mitch clenched his jaw as a familiar ache knotted in his stomach, then settled lower. As much as he loved his mother, as natural as she was with Joey, it wasn't the same as seeing his son in Raine's arms.

Guests arrived. Every aunt, uncle, cousin, neighbor and friend came strolling through the front door. In pairs. The noise level bordered on a deafening roar. Uncle Joe blinded everyone with flashes from his new camera. Cousin Amelia viewed the entire afternoon through the lens of her video camera.

After everyone had made a fuss over Joey, exclaiming how much he looked like the *Harris boys,* Mitch tried to stay out of the way. It worked for a while, but when he saw Uncle Martin approaching, a determined gleam in his eye, Mitch knew he'd been discovered.

Uncle Martin slapped him on the back, and with a jubilant chuckle, began the interrogation. "Still single, eh, boy?" he guffawed, as if Uncle Martin wouldn't have been informed if one of his last three remaining bachelor nephews had taken a wife.

Mitch stole a glance over Martin's shoulder. Kyle and Taylor didn't seem to be faring any better. Aunts Millie and Hazel had them cornered in the living room. He answered Martin's questions as quickly as possible, then excused himself on the pretext of checking on Joey and the caterers. The moment he stepped into the kitchen, a barrage of cousins gathered around him with jokes, more back slaps and still more suggestions. Was there no place to hide?

Joey was getting cranky. With his son and his battered blanket, Mitch took the stairs two at a time, and found himself in the huge bedroom he'd shared with his brothers. He removed Joey's shoes and pulled back the blue spread.

"Where Raine?" the boy asked around his thumb.

Joey's simple question burned in his mind. He'd known his son was attached to Raine, but he'd been so confident everything would work out between them, he hadn't really considered the consequences if she didn't grow to love them both.

Mitch squeezed Joey's little shoulder and said, "Raine's probably at her house back in Allentown."

"Why?"

Mitch knew better than to try to answer Joey's *whys*. This one in particular left him feeling raw. Why was she back in Allentown instead of at his side? Because she didn't love him, or need him or want him.

He sat with Joey until the little boy drifted off to sleep, then went downstairs where he was practically swallowed up into his extremely large family. He somehow managed to duck through a door to the relative safety and peace and quiet of the front porch. Kyle and Taylor were already there, and as Mitch slid his hand into his pocket, he supposed it would always be this way. He and his brothers evidently lacked a vital gene. Without it, they'd remain single. Forever.

The drizzle had let up, but everything looked dark and dismal. It matched his mood. The damp wind blew cold against his skin, but there was no way he was going back inside for his jacket. This kind of weather suited him just fine.

"Where have you been?" Kyle asked.

"I put Joey down for his nap."

"You're going to have to find a mother for that kid," Kyle grumbled. Taylor nodded his head in agreement.

"Sage advice considering neither of you could even get a date for the party today." Realizing how adolescent he sounded, Mitch scowled.

None of them were exactly in talkative moods. Mitch crossed his arms and leaned his back against the cold siding on his parents' house. Laughter and pieces of conversation from the party carried through the wood and glass of the front door.

Kyle grumbled, "If one more person so much as mentions my bachelor status, I swear I'll flatten him. Even Aunt Millie."

Taylor echoed his agreement and Mitch slid his other hand into his pocket where his fingers crinkled the charge statement. No matter how hard he tried to prevent it, his thoughts turned to Raine. He remembered everything about her, the way her eyes twinkled with happiness, the way her hair blew soft and wispy across her forehead. He remembered the way she smiled, the way she walked, the way she laughed. For a normally unobservant person, he'd sure noticed a lot about Raine. They said love changed people. Maybe love had changed him. Or maybe he'd never been unobservant where Raine was concerned.

He wondered if she was over the flu, wondered how she liked her new job and worried about her solo flight. He drew in a deep breath and stared at the row of cars parked along the wet street and driveway. He wanted everyone to leave. He wanted the afternoon to be over. That wasn't all he wanted.

He wanted a chance to love someone, to be loved by that same person. He wanted to have to learn to adjust to the person he loved, like who sleeps on which side of the bed, and whose turn it is to cook dinner or walk the dog. He wanted that person to be Raine. He wanted her to want him in return. He wanted Raine to love him as much as he loved her. He'd hand Raine her freedom on a silver platter if he could, but he couldn't settle for just an honest affair.

The wind filtered through his long-sleeved shirt and seeped beneath his skin, sapping his body heat all the way to his bones. Mitch shivered as he watched a small car turn the corner down the street. He narrowed his eyes and straightened as the vehicle came closer. It looked like Raine's car.

Chapter Eleven

"Who's the cute little number joining the party this late?"

Mitch, who could barely put two thoughts together, didn't know who had asked the question, Kyle or Taylor. All he knew was that Raine had pulled into the driveway, fitting her car into a space almost too small for even her little compact. She'd had him upside down and inside out since the first time he'd laid eyes on her, but it was nothing compared to the way he felt at that moment.

She closed her car door, then began to walk toward the house, her eyes never leaving Mitch's face. He pushed himself from the wall and strode to the porch's top step. There, he hesitated.

On the ride from Allentown, Raine had imagined his reaction to her. She hadn't anticipated his hesitation. She'd noticed the three men standing on the porch the second she'd turned the corner, and had hoped against hope that Mitch would be glad to see her. Uncertainty throbbed through her veins. He didn't look happy to see her. He didn't look happy at all.

She'd unfastened the buttons on her cream-colored wool coat during the drive from Allentown. She didn't take the time to button them now. The wind caught it, billowing the soft fabric behind her, molding her dress to her body. Her heels clicked over the wet concrete, slowing as she neared.

Halfway to Mitch, she stopped. Beneath the intensity of his gaze, she was afraid she'd stumble. Raine swallowed, fighting the trembling in her voice. "What do you do to people who crash your parties?"

She took a tentative step toward him, and Mitch went down to the next step. "I don't know. You're the first person to try it."

She took another step. He did the same. "Why did you?" he asked from the bottom step.

Tears gathered in her eyes. Her gaze strayed to his brothers, who had perked up considerably and were looking from her to Mitch with interest. She wanted to tell him how wrong she'd been, but not in front of an audience. "Is there someplace we can go to talk? Someplace that's private?"

Mitch took another step. Raine watched him cast his brothers a look that said, *get lost, will ya?* They took the hint, but not before they'd slapped him on the back, called him a few choice, brotherly words, then added a wolf whistle or two for good measure.

She was relieved when they finally disappeared inside the house, but when she looked up at Mitch, her sense of relief trailed away. His expression was wary, his emotions hidden. She took a tentative step toward him, all her hopes that he would understand nearly bursting her heart.

He stepped down to the sidewalk, and strode toward her. She met him halfway. The wind whipped her coat behind her, blew her hair off her forehead. Even with the onslaught of the cold breeze, she felt warmed by Mitch's presence.

"Raine, you didn't *have* to come to help."

She felt deflated. What if he really didn't want her here? She hadn't gotten this far in life without developing a little backbone. She straightened her spine and raised her chin as a cold mist began to sift down from the low clouds. It glistened on his face, clung to the waving tendrils of his light brown hair.

"I *did* have to come today, Mitch, but it isn't what you're thinking. I came because I finally realized something while I was flying yesterday. I finally realized—"

"Mitchell Wilfred Harris!"

Raine jerked her head up and looked over Mitch's shoulder. A plump lady with springy gray hair was standing in the open doorway. Her hands were thrust on her ample hips and a stern expression creased her face.

"Wilfred? I thought the *W* stood for Wonderful." At his absentminded expression, she murmured, "I'll explain later."

"Bring your young lady inside, out of the cold this instant!"

Mitch groaned. Not Aunt Millie. For a moment, he'd thought Raine was going to tell him she loved him.

"I think we'd better do as she says, Mitch. She doesn't seem to be the type of woman to tangle with."

Mitch swore under his breath. He took Raine's hand and pulled her toward the house. When they reached the relative protection of the front porch, he fought the desire to swing her into his arms and carry her off. To someplace private, someplace safe. Someplace far away from his overbearing family. If there was even a remote chance that she loved him, he'd rather introduce her to *the mob* in small doses.

But his family never did anything in small doses. The minute he and Raine walked through the front door, they were swallowed into the bosom of his very large, extremely boisterous, incredibly noisy family.

He wanted to get her alone. Instead, he introduced her to his parents. He wanted her to finish her explanation. Instead, Kyle and Taylor swooped down in front of her, introducing themselves as the two *handsome* Harris brothers.

Taylor murmured, ''It seems we've underestimated you, middle brother. You've certainly won the trophy this time.'' He then proceeded to lead Raine away from Mitch's side.

Mitch pulled his hand from his pocket and strode to Raine. If he couldn't beat them, he may as well join them. With a sense of purpose, he clasped her hand firmly in his and led her away from his brothers' clutches.

He'd been worried she'd feel out of place, feel lost in this crowd, but she didn't look either. She raised her face to his and smiled. She seemed to be enjoying the party, and he didn't see a glimmer of obligation in her gaze or in her smile.

Uncle Joe momentarily blinded them as yet another picture was snapped. Mitch introduced Raine to his aunts and uncles. At some point, her coat had been whisked from her shoulders. Cousin Trudy, Millie's firstborn, thrust two plates heaped with food into their hands. ''Now that Mitch has you, maybe you'll take care of him and Joey and make sure they eat right.''

It was all Mitch could do not to dump his plate of food over Trudy's head. He'd spent the past two months trying to prove to Raine that he wasn't one of her responsibilities. It had taken Cousin Trudy less than fifteen seconds to sabotage everything he'd tried to establish.

Mitch hadn't been aware that he'd gritted his teeth and clenched his jaw, until he felt a soft hand glide across his face. His lids lowered, his body reacting to Raine's nearness, to her touch. She was an ever-changing mystery, and for the first time all week, hope began to surge through him.

"We have to talk." With that, he placed both their plates on the table and pulled her with him to the front closet where he rummaged around for their coats. After several minutes, he slipped hers over her shoulders, then gave up trying to find his. Without letting go of her hand, he kept her tight to his side until they were once again alone on the front porch.

"Mitch, you have a very unusual family."

"Did you drive all the way from Allentown to talk about my family?"

"No." She turned to face him.

"There you two are!" Cousin Trudy crowed. "I wondered where you'd gone."

Without saying a word, Mitch and Raine both turned and skipped down the porch steps, leaving Cousin Trudy with her mouth gaping while they wended their way between the cars lining the driveway. At her car's front bumper, they stopped.

It had begun to drizzle again, but neither seemed to notice. She squared her shoulders and faced him. With only inches separating them, she murmured, "I came to your party..."

"Raine, how many times have I—"

"...because I love you." Tears clouded her vision but she was certain she hadn't imagined the powerful emotion in Mitch's eyes. "I love you. I think I always have. I just didn't know how much until yesterday. I'm so sorry I hurt you. I thought loving you would tie me down, but loving you has set me free."

Before she could do anything, his arms wound around her back beneath her coat. She held on for dear life as he swung her off her feet, spinning them both in a circle. The instant her feet found the ground, she raised her face to his and touched her lips to his. He pulled her to him, wrapping her tight in his embrace.

She felt the cold of his hands through the soft fabric of her dress. "You're shivering," she murmured.

His voice was husky and incredibly deep with pent-up emotion. "I've been cold without you."

Her eyelids lowered with feeling. Raising her gaze to his, she whispered, "And I've been empty without you."

Shrill wolf whistles and catcalls rent the air. Kyle and Taylor and several of their male cousins were at it again. Raine and Mitch both smiled, but those sounds didn't filter through the cloud that seemed to encircle them. She kissed him with total abandon, giving herself freely to the passion in his touch.

His chest heaved with labored breathing. "Let's find a place where you can warm me and I can fill your emptiness."

Anticipation lowered her eyelids and love filled her heart. The distant wolf whistles filtered into their private world. "Kyle and Taylor?"

He nodded. "Completely juvenile."

"Don't talk about my future brothers-in-law that way."

"Are you asking?"

"Unless you'd rather."

"You're sure?"

With a deep-seated conviction, Raine knew she had to find the words to convince him of her love, of her need. That conviction steadied her voice. "I've never been more sure about anything in my entire life. I want to live with you, love with you, share with you. I want to raise Joey as my own son, and someday give him a brother or sister."

He started to speak, but she touched his lips with her finger, then wrapped her coat around them both. "I finally realized what I needed while I was flying that plane yesterday. I finally realized I'll only be free if you're by my side."

When he framed her face with his hands, she felt him already beginning to warm. Lowering his mouth to hers, he swept her into his arms and strode to her little car. He slowly slid her down his body until her feet touched the driveway. The look in his eyes made her bold. With a husky voice, she whispered, "You haven't mentioned my hair."

"Your hair?" he asked.

"I had it trimmed yesterday. Right after I bought my new license plate. I wanted everything to be perfect for today."

Mitch looked at the front of her car. In bright blue letters, the words *I Love My Dentist* practically jumped from the plate. He reached for her, then tucked a strand of soft blond hair behind her ear. His gaze roamed over her face as his fingers brushed through the tendrils at her temple.

The hair waving over her collar didn't look shorter to him, but the tresses feathering her face were no longer in her eyes. "You look so *fine.*"

Her senses soared with his compliment, though more from the look in his eyes and from the velvety texture of his voice than from his words. She knew she'd never mind the word *fine* again.

Mitch reached into his pocket as if searching for his keys. His hand came up with the charge bill. Raine took it from his fingers, then glanced over the items. With a woman's smile, she murmured, "I'm wearing something else from Leslie Anne's Boutique."

Mitch pressed a kiss to her temple before groaning out loud. "That settles it. We have to get out of here."

"What about Joey?"

Mitch shook his head. She'd done it to him again, made him forget his own flesh and blood, made him forget his own name, made him forget everything except the promise in her eyes.

"He's asleep upstairs. We still have two hours before he wakes up."

Aunt Millie's petulant voice demanded their attention. "Come back inside, both of you. Mitchell! This occasion is extremely important to your parents."

"Oh, can it, Millie," Mitch's father grumbled from the front porch. It seemed everyone was watching, either from the porch or from the windows and doorways. Cousin Amelia had captured the entire episode on her video camera.

Mitch groaned again. "You're right about my family," he sputtered. "They really are strange."

"You two go on," his mother called. "Thanks for everything, Mitch. I'm so happy to meet you, Raine. I'm glad you could join us today and I'm looking forward to seeing you again."

Before anyone moved, Raine called, "We'll be back for Joey in a little while." Spreading her arms wide to encompass everyone, she added, "I'm looking forward to knowing all of you, too."

Mitch's mother proceeded to usher the onlookers back inside, but not before Millie sputtered, "I declare! It looks like there's going to be another wedding in the family."

Mitch maneuvered the little car out of the tight parking space and Raine waved to her future in-laws. She took the crinkled charge bill from his right hand and began to laugh. "I think we have to talk about your taste in women's clothing."

Her laughter warmed him all the way down to his soul. He cast her his most decadent look and kissed her on the mouth, somehow managing to keep the car between the lines on the highway. "You haven't seen anything yet."

The promise in his voice filled the emptiness in her heart.

Slowly, the laughter seeped out of her. It was replaced with warm, cherished feelings, feelings that welled up inside her until she was brimming with happiness. "I love you, Mitchell Wilfred Harris."

"I know. And I love you."

Raine smiled at his smug expression. The car crested another hill, then sped down the other side. With love uniting them like clasped hands, she and Mitch soared into their future, together.

Is another Harris brother going to give up his bachelor status? Watch for Kyle's story,
BACHELOR AT THE WEDDING, coming soon from Silhouette Romance.

* * * * *

Dark secrets, dangerous desire...

Lovers DARK AND DANGEROUS

Three spine-tingling tales from the dark side of love.

This October, enter the world of shadowy romance as Silhouette presents the third in their annual tradition of thrilling love stories and chilling story lines. Written by three of Silhouette's top names:

LINDSAY McKENNA
LEE KARR
RACHEL LEE

Haunting a store near you this October.

HE'S MORE THAN A MAN,
HE'S ONE OF OUR

MAIL-ORDER BROOD
Arlene James

Leon Paradise was shocked when he discovered that his mail-order bride came with a ready-made family. No sooner had he said his vows when a half-dozen kids showed up on his doorstep. Now the handsome rancher had to decide if his home—and his heart—were big enough for Cassie Esterbridge *and* the brood she'd brought into his life.

Look for *Mail-Order Brood* by Arlene James.
Available in August.
Fall in love with our **Fabulous Fathers!**

R O M A N C E™

FF894

The Loop™

Is the future what it's cracked up to be?

This August, find out how C. J. Clarke copes with being on her own in

GETTING IT TOGETHER: CJ
by Wendy Corsi Staub

Her diet was a flop. Her "beautiful" apartment was cramped. Her "glamour" job consisted of fetching coffee. And her love life was less than zero. But what C.J. didn't know was that things were about to get better....

The ups and downs of modern life continue with

GETTING IT RIGHT: JESSICA
by Carla Cassidy in September

GETTING REAL: CHRISTOPHER
by Kathryn Jensen in October

Get smart. Get into "The Loop!"

Only from ▼ *Silhouette*® ™

where passion lives.

Fifty red-blooded, white-hot, true-blue hunks
from every State in the Union!

Look for MEN MADE IN AMERICA! Written by some of
our most popular authors, these stories feature fifty of
the strongest, sexiest men, each from a different state in
the union!

Two titles available every month at your favorite retail
outlet.

In August, look for:

PROS AND CONS by Bethany Campbell
(Massachusetts)
TO TAME A WOLF by Anne McAllister (Michigan)

In September, look for:

WINTER LADY by Janet Joyce (Minnesota)
AFTER THE STORM by Rebecca Flanders (Mississippi)

You won't be able to resist MEN MADE IN AMERICA!

▼ *Silhouette* ROMANCE™

**First comes marriage.... Will love follow?
Find out this September when Silhouette Romance
presents**

Join six couples who marry for convenient reasons, and still
find happily-ever-afters. Look for these wonderful books by
some of your favorite authors:

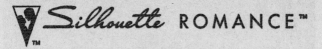

Silhouette ROMANCE™

presents

TIMELY MATRIMONY
by
Kasey Michaels

Suzi Harper found Harry Wilde on a storm-swept beach. But this handsome time traveler from the nineteenth century needed more than a rescuer—he needed a bride to help him survive the modern world. Suzi may have been a willing wife, but could a man from the past be a husband for all time?

Look for *Timely Matrimony* in September, featured in our month of

Hasty Weddings

SRKM